Dream Catcher

Maria Iskander

Maria Iskander

DREAM CATCHER

© Maria Iskander

ISBN: 978-1-7644772-0-8 Paperback

ISBN: 978-1-7644772-1-5 E-Book

First Published January 2026

Published with the assistance of Angel Key Publications
https://angelkey.com.au

Contents

Dedication

For the late Elijah, late Pete, and late Chief Billy. Your agape friendship was 'elementally' inspired. Please keep us all in your prayers

Author's Note

Thank you for joining Yos on his journey—a story of dreams, truth, and the courage to stand apart in a world that often silences what it does not understand.

This book began with a simple question: *What if our dreams were more than private imaginations? What if they were a moral compass, guiding us not toward power or escape, but toward understanding, empathy, and purpose?* Yos's story is a meditation on that idea. His trials—exile, betrayal, and despair—mirror the moments in all our lives when the world seems unfair, when hope feels distant, and when we doubt our own voice. Yet, even in darkness, dreams—literal or metaphorical—remind us that truth and light persist.

The city Yos inhabits, both luminous and mechanical, reflects our own world: a place full of complexity, technology, ambition, and the delicate balance between control and freedom. Through Yos, Mara, and the people he touches, I wanted to explore what it means to belong, to forgive, and to act with integrity when the stakes are high.

At its heart, this is a story about listening—to our own hearts, to the dreams of others, and to the quiet guidance that life provides. Dreams are fragile, but they are powerful. They do not promise safety, wealth, or ease. They promise truth. And that truth, when embraced, can illuminate the path through the darkest nights.

If there is one thought I hope you carry with you after turning the final page, it is this: *Even when the world silences you, your truth still speaks. And sometimes, following it is the most extraordinary adventure you will ever undertake.*

Thank you for dreaming alongside Yos. May you listen to your own dreams, and may they guide you—not to an escape, but to the courage, compassion, and purpose that make life worth living.

With gratitude,
Maria Iskander.

Epigraph

"They said, 'Here comes the dreamer.'
Let us see what will become of his dreams."
— Genesis 37:19–20

Prologue

The Language of Light

They say dreams are just noise —

the mind sorting through static,

the heart trying to make sense of itself.

But I've always believed dreams speak in another
language.

Not of words or logic,

but of symbols that glimmer at the edge of morning —

a river that never stops moving,

a voice that never stops calling.

When I was a kid, I used to tell my brothers what I saw
at night.

Sometimes they laughed.

Sometimes they grew quiet,

like they'd touched something too sacred to name.

I thought light meant safety back then.

I didn't know it could also mean exposure —

how it reveals everything,

even the things you wish it wouldn't.

The first time I lost everything,

I didn't fall into darkness.

I fell into silence —

a silence so wide it could swallow whole galaxies.

And still, somewhere inside that stillness,

a dream was waiting for me.

Not a promise.

Not a prophecy.

Just a whisper:

"Keep believing. Even here."

So that's what I did.

And maybe that's what this story really is —

not about the rise, or the fall,

or the moments when the world almost forgot me.

It's about the quiet in-between.

The space where faith becomes real.

The moment the dreamer stops dreaming

and starts to wake up.

Part 1 — The Dreamer

(Before the fall)

I saw the sky fold into rivers of light,
and every star bent low,
whispering my name like a secret it had kept too long.

When I woke, the world was quieter —
as if it, too, was listening.

(Symbol: Innocence, calling, the foreshadow of destiny.)

Opening Image

The rooftop was the only place that still felt like his.

A square of cracked concrete, stained by forgotten rain and the shadows of a broken railing, hovering twelve stories above Alexandria, an Egyptian city that never learned how to whisper. Below, traffic moaned, neon signs hummed, people barked the edges of their lives into each other—but up here, at the very edge of night, it was possible to pretend the noise was a distant ocean rather than the grinding machinery of living.

Yos sat cross-legged near the rusted access door, his journal opens on his lap, the pages bowing in the soft winter breeze. A cheap pen, bitten at the cap, hovered above the paper. He waited for the words to come like he always did. Patient, uncertain, as though Yos didn't want to frighten them.

The city lights washed over him—puddles of gold, blue, pink, and that strange violet glow from the holo-ads downtown. The colours mixed on the surface of his journal, shimmering on his fingertips like small, hesitant promises.

He inhaled deeply. Not for courage. For stillness.

His dream still clung to him, fragile and persistent, like the aftertaste of something sweet he wasn't ready to let go of.

Tonight, he wrote.

Alexandria was a city of light. Light that wasn't loud, somehow.

Light that didn't want anything from me.

He paused, listening to the wind push against the metal staircase behind him. The rooftop creaked in response, as if acknowledging his presence.

He pressed his pen harder.

Everything glowed. Streets, rooftops, even the sky like someone had gently cracked it open. And there was silence. Not emptiness—silence like a held breath, like meaning waiting its turn. I wasn't afraid.

His writing slowed. He looked up, letting the real city blur into the imagined one.

In his dream, he'd stood alone in the middle of a vast intersection. Every building shone from within, as if the people inside had transformed into lanterns. Light poured out of windows, spilled down fire escapes, trickled across the asphalt in rivers of warm colour. Yet everything was still—no engines, no voices, no electric tantrums of billboards advertising better lives.

Just quiet radiance.

In waking life, silence was a rare animal. Hard to catch. Harder to keep.

He exhaled and continued scribbling.

The silence didn't feel like losing sound; it felt like finding myself. It was the first time I heard my thoughts clearly. My truth didn't have to compete.

A helicopter thudded somewhere to the south, a repetitive mechanical heartbeat shredding the thin curtain of calm around him. Yos winced, drawing his knees tighter to his chest. The wind lifted a corner of the journal page; he pinned it with his thumb.

He'd always felt too loud on the inside and too quiet on the outside, like the world had been tuned to the wrong frequency for him. People expected noise, confidence, volume—things he'd never learned or, if he was honest, never wanted. Still, loneliness carved its shape into him, day by day. Being different wasn't the hard part. Being unseen was.

Maybe that was why the dream mattered so much. A city full of light and silence felt like a promise that there might be a place where he belonged simply by existing.

He pressed the pen again.

In that dream, I wasn't trying to be understood. I already was.

The lights below flickered as a passing cloud dimmed the moon. Yos watched the shift, fascinated by how quickly brightness surrendered to shade. That fleeting dimness reminded him of the moment right before waking—when the dream had started dissolving around him.

The silence had gone first.

Not shattered, not broken—just faded, like someone slowly turning a dial. Then the light dimmed, leaking away until he stood in a patch of darkness that grew heavier by the second. Anxiety had crawled up his spine, tightening around his throat. Alexandria, his home, was leaving him. Or he was being pulled away from it. He couldn't tell which was worse.

He had tried to stay, reaching for a streetlamp that glowed like a warm hand, but time in dreams is uncooperative. His fingers had passed right through the light, and the moment they did, he woke up in his bed with the window rattling from the morning traffic below.

Now, sitting on the rooftop under the real moon, he tried to reclaim whatever the dream had tried to give him.

Maybe the light wasn't the point, he wrote. Maybe it was the silence. A place where I didn't need to speak to be known. A place where I wasn't too much or not enough. Just…me. Maybe that's what I'm looking for.

He tapped the pen on the journal, thinking.

Below him, a siren began its climb, wailing upward like Alexandria hated the idea of quiet. Yos tilted his head back, eyes tracing the shape of a distant skyscraper whose top floors blinked with red aviation lights.

He wondered if anyone else in the whole city ever craved silence the way he did—longed for it like a person yearns for touch.

The breeze shifted from cold to colder, brushing over his hair and carrying the faint smell of fried food from a vendor on the street below. Yos shivered and zipped up his jacket, but he didn't move to go inside. The rooftop was the only place he could breathe without feeling like he owed something to someone.

Sometimes I think the world is allergic to quiet. It sneezes noise everywhere. People try to shout their truth over each other, but all that shouting just makes everything blur together. Maybe that's why I don't speak much. Not because I have nothing to say, but because I don't want my voice to be another blur.

He paused, letting the words settle.

But dreams aren't bound by that. In dreams, the world listens. Even when the world silences you, your truth still speaks.

His pen scratched the final sentence with unusual confidence. He liked the way it looked on the page—simple, unashamed.

The wind fluttered his hair again, almost playfully, and for a moment he imagined the rooftop itself reading over his shoulder, nodding in agreement.

He wondered what it would be like if Alexandria, could listen that way. If people could feel each other's truths without all the noise between them. If belonging could happen without performance.

Under the moonlight, surrounded by the glow of careless neon, he allowed himself the tiniest hope that maybe he wasn't as alone as he felt.

Even a dream had reached for him.

The hour grew later; the city lights sharpened as the night deepened. Somewhere, a distant train groaned like a tired animal. Yos flipped back through the journal pages he'd filled tonight—about the dream, the silence, the light that didn't demand anything.

He let his fingers rest on the ink, feeling the texture of his own thoughts pressed into paper.

For the first time all day, he didn't feel invisible.

His truth, quiet as it was, lived here in these lines. He belonged at least to this rooftop, to this moment, to the part of himself brave enough to write.

Yos looked up at the sky. The cloud that had dimmed the moon drifted away, revealing a soft glow spreading across the night like diluted milk. It reminded him of the dream-a light gentler than neon, patient, and listening.

He closed his journal but kept it in his hands, warm against his palms.

Maybe he couldn't find silence in the waking world, not the way he craved it. But he could make something like it. In writing. In dreaming. In the way he paid attention to things most people ignored.

That was its own kind of belonging.

He stood, stretching stiff legs, and walked to the edge of the rooftop. Alexandria sprawled beneath him, loud and luminous and utterly unaware. Yet despite its noise, he felt a fragile ribbon of hope unfurl inside him.

Even when the world silences you, he repeated silently,

your truth still speaks.

And on this rooftop, under this moon, he believed it.

Theme Stated

Morning crept into Yos's room reluctantly, as if it knew he wasn't ready for it. Thin gold light leaked between the blinds and stretched itself across the floorboards, touching the scattered notebooks like someone riffling through his secrets.

Yos blinked awake slowly, the last notes of the dream still echoing in his chest. The memory felt fragile now, dissolving with every heartbeat. He reached for his journal on the bedside table—not to write, but to reassure himself the words from last night were still there, tangible proof that the dream had existed.

Through the wall, he heard the low hum of the kitchen appliances, followed by the uneven thump-thump of his father's footsteps—always a little heavier in the mornings, like the day hadn't fully settled into his bones yet.

Yos rolled out of bed and tugged on yesterday's sweater. The hallway smelled faintly of coffee and burnt toast. His father was terrible with bread; he insisted every toaster in the world was "mis-calibrated."

Yos turned the corner into the kitchen just as his father was scraping the blackened edge of a toast slice into the sink.

"Morning," his father said without looking up, his voice gravel warm.

"Morning," Yos answered, voice soft from sleep.

His father finally glanced at him—and paused. "You're thinking hard already. It's barely sunrise."

Yos shrugged, sliding into a chair. "Just…dream stuff."

His father grunted knowingly, as though that explained everything.

Yos's father wasn't a man who believed in small talk, so the silence that followed wasn't awkward—it was familiar. Comfortable, even. The kind of silence Yos wished the rest of the world understood.

His father set a mug of tea in front of him. Yos cupped it in both hands, feeling the steam warm his nose. He waited for the right words, but they tangled in his throat.

"I had a dream," Yos finally said. "A strong one."

His father leaned against the counter; arms crossed. "You have lots of dreams."

"Not like this," Yos insisted. His fingers tightened around the ceramic. "The whole of Alexandria was glowing. Quiet. Not empty quiet—just…peaceful quiet. Like the world remembered how to breathe."

His father's expression didn't change, but something softened around the edges of his eyes. He knew Yos well enough to recognize when a dream meant something more than just passing night-thoughts.

"You think it means something?" he asked.

Yos nodded. "I don't know what, though. But I keep thinking about it. About how I felt inside it. Like I wasn't getting pulled in a hundred directions. Like everything finally…fit."

His father walked over and pulled out the chair across from him. The scrape of wood on floor was the only harsh sound in the room.

"You've always lived with one foot in the dream world," his father said. "Sometimes I think you trust your dreams more than you trust yourself."

Yos looked down. He wasn't sure if that was a criticism or an observation.

"Is that bad?" he asked quietly.

His father chuckled under his breath. "Not necessarily."

Steam curled upward from his father's coffee in soft spirals. He watched it for a moment, as though waiting for it to finish a thought before speaking.

"Dreams are important," his father said. "We need them. They're like…compasses we keep inside our ribs. They point us toward who we could become."

Yos lifted his gaze. "So you think dreams show us the future?"

His father shook his head. "No. They show us ourselves."

The words lingered in the air, warm and weighty. Yos felt a small stirring inside his chest, something equal parts curiosity and fear.

His father continued; voice steady but gentle. "But listen carefully, Yos. Dreams aren't for escaping life." He met Yos's eyes fully now, holding them. "They're for shaping it."

There it was. The sentence that felt like someone had quietly placed a key in Yos's hand.

Yos swallowed. The words struck him somewhere deep, behind the ribs, where last night's dream had settled like a soft, persistent echo. Shaping life. Not hiding from it.

His thoughts felt suddenly too loud, colliding in his mind like startled birds.

"I don't think I'm trying to escape," Yos managed, though he wasn't completely sure.

His father tilted his head. "Maybe not consciously. But when the world feels overwhelming, dreams can look like doorways. Easy exits." He tapped the table. "But the real power is when you use them as entrances instead."

Yos frowned slightly. "Entrances to what?"

"To whom you're meant to be."

The words sank slowly, the way ink spreads across paper. Yos stared at the kitchen table, tracing a scratch in the wood with his fingertip. His father wasn't one for philosophizing—when he said something that sounded like wisdom, it usually meant he'd been thinking about it for a long time.

"So what do I do with it?" Yos asked in a small voice. "The dream?"

"Well," his father said, rubbing his jaw thoughtfully, "first you figure out why it matters to you. Not what it means in some mystical sense. Why you felt it so strongly."

Yos considered that. The quiet. The light. The feeling of belonging without having to perform or explain. The sense of understanding without being seen through. It was like the dream had been the version of the world he wished existed.

He cleared his throat. "I guess…it felt like what I want the real world to be like. At least a little."

"Then that's where you start," his father replied. "A dream that shows you what you want? That's not an escape. That's direction."

Yos felt his chest tighten again—but not painfully this time. More like something unfolding.

"Dad?"

"Hm?"

"Do you ever have dreams like that?"

His father smiled, slow and nostalgic. "Once. When I was about your age. It told me I wanted to build things that made people feel safer. That's why I became an engineer, you know."

Yos blinked. He'd never heard that story before. His father didn't talk much about himself.

"Did it work?" Yos asked quietly.

His father looked out the window, as if checking the answer against the skyline. "I like to think so."

Yos let the tea sit between his palms until the surface cooled.

"Dreams as compasses," he repeated under his breath. "Not doors."

His father raised a brow. "Exactly."

Yos nodded slowly, storing the idea away like a precious stone he wasn't ready to examine fully yet.

He thought of the dream again—of the glowing buildings, of the silence that felt like being understood without speaking. If that was a compass, what was it pointing him toward? A life with quieter? More truth? More…being himself?

The idea terrified him.

But it also felt right.

His father stood, stretching his shoulders until they cracked. "If that dream meant something, you'll figure it out. You always do. Just don't use it to hide from the world. Use it to step into it."

Yos looked up sharply. "Step into it? But I don't even know where to step."

His father chuckled. "That's the thing about compasses, kiddo. They don't show you the whole map. Just the direction."

Yos let the words settle over him like a blanket.

"Okay," he said softly. "I'll…try."

"That's all anyone can ask."

His father walked to the sink to rinse his mug, humming a tune Yos didn't recognize. The morning light had thickened, coating the kitchen in a warm yellow sheen. It made everything feel a little softer, like the day was offering forgiveness before anything had even gone wrong.

Yos stood and moved to the doorway but paused.

"Dad?"

His father glanced back.

"Thanks."

A small smile tugged at the corner of his father's

mouth. "Anytime."

Yos stepped into the hallway with the journal tucked under his arm. His father's words echoed through him, aligning with the remnants of the dream until they formed something new—something steady, like a pulse.

Dreams aren't for escaping life. They're for shaping it.

If that was true, then maybe the dream wasn't just a place he wished existed. Maybe it was a reminder. A calling. A direction pointing inward and forward at the same time.

He didn't know what it meant yet.

But for the first time, not knowing didn't feel like failure.

It felt like beginning.

Set-Up

The day unfolded slowly, as if carrying the weight of his father's words.

Yos wandered into the living room, rubbing the sleep from his eyes. Sunlight spilled through the windows in buttery stripes, catching the dust motes dancing above the old couch. He heard the telltale sound of tension before he saw its source—the low murmur of Kamal's irritation, the sharp rustle of Rafi's sarcasm, the uneasy silence of Dany caught between them.

His brothers rarely started the morning without disagreement. Today was no exception.

Kamal, broad-shouldered and eternally simmering, stood by the TV with his arms crossed over his chest like a barricade. Rafi lounged on the armchair, picking at the threads of the fabric as though unravelling it served some private purpose. And Dany—tallest but somehow the smallest—sat perched on the edge of a stool, shoulders curled inward like he expected something heavy to fall.

Kamal snorted when he saw Yos. "Look who decided to grace us with his presence."

Rafi smirked without looking up. "Dream prince returns."

Dany lifted a hand in a small greeting, the most genuine of the three.

Yos offered a quiet, "Morning."

Kamal rolled his eyes. "He talks. Amazing."

Yos didn't respond. He'd learned that words were wasted on Kamal before noon.

Their father entered a moment later, wiping his hands on a dish towel. His face brightened when he saw Yos—just slightly, but enough for the room to feel it. Enough for his brothers to notice.

"Yos," their father said warmly, "I fixed the zipper on your hoodie. Left it on your bed."

The shift was instant. Kamal's jaw tightened. Rafi stilled. Dany looked down, guilt blooming behind his eyes like a bruise.

Yos felt his stomach tighten. Here we go.

The hoodie wasn't special—not at first. It was just navy blue, soft, warm. But it had become a symbol months ago when their father gave it to him unexpectedly after a long week of exams. A subtle gesture, but meaningful. Too meaningful.

His brothers hadn't forgotten.

"Of course he fixed your hoodie," Kamal muttered. "Mine's been ripped for months."

"You ripped yours in a fight," Rafi reminded him. "Hard to fix stupidity."

"Say that again," Kamal snapped, stepping toward him.

"Please don't," Dany whispered.

Yos said nothing. The tension wasn't his fault, but he felt responsible anyway—something he was good at feeling, even without cause.

Their father sighed. "I'll fix yours too, Kamal. I told you that. I just…haven't had time."

"Right," Kamal said, voice dripping with disbelief. "But time for Yos. Always time for Yos."

The accusation hung in the air like smoke.

The moment dragged. Their father opened his mouth, closed it, reopened it again—looking older than he had in months.

"It wasn't like that," he said quietly. "Yos just needed—"

"What? More than us?" Kamal barked.

Rafi's smirk returned, bitter and sharp. "He always needs more."

Dany winced. "Guys…please."

Yos stood there, hands at his sides, knowing anything he said would only stoke the flames. So, he swallowed the familiar guilt and simply nodded once, hoping the gesture would soften the moment.

It didn't.

His father's shoulders sagged. He looked at his eldest sons with something between exhaustion and sorrow.

"We'll talk about this later," he said.

Kamal scoffed and stormed toward the hallway. Rafi followed, muttering something Yos didn't catch.
Dany lingered for a moment, offering Yos a helpless, apologetic look before trailing after them.

The house felt hollow once they were gone.

His father turned to him, rubbing the bridge of his nose.

"Yos," he said, "don't take that to heart. They…they're dealing with their own things."

Yos nodded automatically. He knew the line by heart.

"They just care differently," his father added, forcing a weak smile.

"Yeah," Yos murmured. "I know."

But a part of him wondered—quietly, dangerously—if being cared for differently was just a polite way of admitting he didn't fit. Not with his brothers. Not with their heat, their noise, their jagged edges. He loved them, but their love felt like a storm he was always caught outside of.

His father rested a hand briefly on his shoulder. "You're not the problem, Yos."

Yos wanted to believe him.

Needed to.

But belief felt heavy today.

The Hoodie

Later, in his room, Yos found the hoodie folded neatly on his bed, centered as if someone had taken care to place it just right. The fabric was smooth, the creases clean. The zipper caught the light from the window, glinting silver—freshly repaired, its teeth aligned again like nothing had ever been wrong.

Almost new.

He stood there for a moment without touching it.
Just looked.

The hoodie had been with him through things he didn't name out loud—late nights, long silences, the kind of days that left him hollowed out but still moving. It wasn't special to anyone else. To them, it was just clothing. To him, it was something closer to proof.

Yos picked it up and pressed it to his chest.

The fabric was warm already, holding the faintest trace of heat, as if it remembered him. He breathed in before he realized he was doing it. Laundry soap—clean, soft—but underneath that, something else. Something familiar and steady. He could never put a word to it.

Comfort, maybe.

His fingers curled into the sleeves. He loved the hoodie—not because it meant something grand or symbolic, but because when he wore it, his body seemed to unclench on its own. Like it knew it was allowed to rest.

But wearing it around his brothers felt like walking into a fire with gasoline.

They didn't have to say anything. The looks were enough. The jokes, the sharp grins, the way silence could turn heavy and pointed. The hoodie invited comments. Questions. Assumptions. It softened him in ways they noticed and never let go unchallenged.

Yos swallowed.

He could leave it on the bed. Fold it back up. Choose something safer—something invisible.

Still…

He pulled it over his head.

The fabric slid down his arms, settled against his shoulders. The zipper rested at his sternum, cool for a second before warming. As soon as it touched him fully, something subtle shifted inside his ribs—like a door opening just enough to let air in.

It felt like stepping into the version of himself he wished he could be more often.

Quiet, yes—but not diminished. Thoughtful. Present. Soft in a world that demanded hard edges and louder voices.

He caught his reflection in the darkened window. Hood down, eyes steady. The hoodie didn't change him. It didn't make him braver or stronger.

It just let him be.

Yos pulled the hood up, letting it frame his face, dim the room a little. The noise of the house faded to a distant hum—the clatter of dishes, a voice raised in laughter, footsteps passing his door.

He exhaled.

For a moment, held inside fabric and breath and warmth, he felt intact.

Mara

School corridors were loud in a way that made Yos feel invisible. Everyone spoke at once, each voice trying to overpower the others—a chorus of small, desperate performances. Lockers slammed. Laughter ricocheted. Sneakers squeaked against the floor.

He moved through it all quietly, backpack tight against his shoulders, hoodie zipped up like a boundary. No one looked at him long enough to see him.

And then—

Mara found him anyway.

She always did.

She slipped beside him near the lockers, walking with an easy stride that matched his pace without needing to ask. No sudden movements. No awkward adjustments. Just presence.

Mara had a kind of gentle confidence that made her seem like she belonged to every room she entered. Not loud, not demanding—simply certain. Her dark curls were tied loosely, strands already falling free, brushing her cheeks when she smiled.

"You look tired," she said, nudging his shoulder with hers. "Dream binge again?"

Yos felt his shoulders loosen without thinking.

"Kind of," he said. "It was…a big one."

"Big how?"

He hesitated, then shrugged. "It felt like a message."

She grinned, unbothered. "Your dreams always feel like messages."

"That's the problem," he murmured, eyes on the floor as they walked.

Mara slowed just a fraction so he had to look at her.

"No," she said softly. "That's what I like about you."

He blinked, caught off guard. She kept going, like it was the simplest truth in the world.

"Most people think dreams are random noise," she said. "You think they mean something. You see meaning everywhere, Yos. That's rare. Don't stop."

Her words pulled something warm through him, like sunlight breaking across cold water—slow, quiet, undeniable.

"Thanks," he whispered, the word small but full.

She bumped his shoulder again, lighter this time. "Anytime."

The bell rang somewhere down the hall, sharp and insistent. Students surged around them.

But for a moment longer, Yos didn't feel invisible at all.

Rafi Watches

What neither of them noticed was Rafi leaning against the lockers at the far end of the hall.

He stood half in shadow, arms folded tight across his chest, one shoulder pressed into cold metal. Students passed him without pause—laughing, shoving, shouting over one another—but Rafi didn't move. His expression was unreadable, carved into something flat and controlled.

He watched Yos and Mara walk together down the corridor.

Too close. Too easy.

Rafi's gaze caught first on the hoodie.

That stupid hoodie.

It stood out against the chaos of the hallway—soft, muted, unmistakably his. Something in Rafi's jaw tightened as he tracked it, the familiar spike of irritation flaring before he could stop it. He hated the thing without ever naming why. Maybe because it made Yos look protected. Maybe because it made him look like someone worth protecting.

Rafi's eyes slid from the hoodie to Yos's face.

Then to Mara.

They were laughing—not loudly, not for show. Just enough to belong to each other. Mara leaned in slightly as she spoke, her steps matching Yos's without effort. No performance. No edge.

Rafi felt something twist, slow and sharp, just beneath his ribs.

"Unbelievable," he muttered under his breath.

The word tasted bitter.

The jealousy wasn't simple. It never was. It wasn't even about Mara—at least, not entirely. He told himself that, over and over, as if repetition might make it true.

It was about Yos's ease.

The way people softened around him. The way he listened like it mattered. The way sincerity came to him naturally, as if he'd never learned how dangerous it was to let others see you clearly.

Rafi had learned early.

Rafi was clever. Sharp. He knew how to speak so people laughed—or backed off. He knew how to win arguments, how to keep control.

And yet—

Yos, who didn't even try, pulled people in.

Rafi's fingers flexed against his arms, nails biting lightly through his sleeves. He watched until Yos and Mara disappeared into the crush of bodies near the stairwell, the space they left behind somehow louder for their absence.

Something in his chest burned.

He shoved off the lockers and kicked one shut as he passed. The clang rang out too loud, earning him a glance from a nearby teacher, but Rafi didn't slow down. He didn't look back.

As he walked away, resentment followed him like a shadow—stretching long and dark behind every step.

And somewhere beneath it, buried deep enough to deny, was a quieter thought he refused to face:

Why him?

Transition

As Rafi disappeared down the hall, the echo of the locker's clang faded—but the feeling it left behind did not. It lingered, heavy and unresolved, like a held breath that never quite released.

That night, Yos carried the weight home with him without knowing why.

It settled into his bones as he lay in bed, the house quiet, the hoodie folded within reach. His thoughts drifted, unguarded, slipping past the edges of waking. The day unraveled into fragments—Mara's voice, the corridor noise, a sense of being seen from somewhere he couldn't name.

And then sleep took him.

Not gently.

The dream came.

The Dream of Stars

That night, the dream came.

Not the way his dreams usually did—slipping in softly, half-formed and half-forgotten—but all at once, whole and undeniable, as if it had been waiting patiently for him to close his eyes.

This one was different.

Yos found himself standing in a vast, dark field, emptier than any place he'd ever been. There was no wind, no sound, no smell—nothing to anchor him. The silence pressed in, complete and absolute.

The ground beneath his feet was smooth black glass. It reflected the sky perfectly, so flawlessly that the horizon dissolved. He couldn't tell where the world ended and heaven began. Above and below mirrored each other, trapping him between two infinities.

He looked down at his feet.

They were solid. He was real.

That, somehow, made the emptiness heavier.

Above him, the stars began to move.

At first it was subtle—a slow drifting, like embers lifted by a distant current. Then the motion sharpened, purposeful. The stars swept across the sky in wide arcs, gathering together, tightening into a vast spiral that turned and turned, drawing closer with every breath Yos took.

He felt the pull in his chest.

Not fear. Not urgency.

Recognition.

Without thinking, Yos lifted his hand.

The stars reacted immediately. Their spinning slowed, the spiral loosening as if the sky itself were reconsidering. One by one, the lights hesitated—then drifted downward, falling gently toward his open palm.

The air hummed.

One star touched his skin.

The instant it did, the sky erupted with light.

The light wasn't blinding. It didn't overwhelm him.

It welcomed him.

Warmth spread outward in waves, like thousands of quiet voices sighing in relief all at once. The darkness softened, retreating as the stars flared brighter. They rearranged themselves deliberately, forming constellations Yos had never seen before.

Not creatures. Not legends.

Paths.

Lines of possibility. Shapes of direction. They pointed forward and outward, offering answers without words, purpose without command.

Yos felt himself lift.

His feet left the glass without resistance. The ground didn't shatter or vanish—it simply let him go. He rose slowly, weightless, as though the universe had reached a quiet conclusion and chosen him for something unfinished.

For the first time in the dream, Yos felt certain.

He was meant to be here.

The certainty shattered behind him.

A sharp crack split the horizon, violent and sudden. The mirrored sky fractured like broken ice, darkness bleeding through the wound. The stars nearest the rupture flickered, their steady glow stuttering.

Three figures emerged.

At first, they were only shadows—elongated and distorted by the broken light. Then they sharpened as they stepped forward onto the fractured glass.

His brothers.

Kamal.

Rafi.

Dany.

They stood together, watching him rise. Their faces were lit by the faltering stars, their eyes burning with something fierce and unmistakable.

Not awe.

Not pride.

Jealousy.

Fear.

Bitterness.

The dream twisted.

The stars trembled, their constellations shuddering out of alignment. The warm light dimmed, growing heavy, as if doubt itself had weight. Yos felt the pull reverse, dragging at his chest.

His brothers reached for him.

Not to follow.

Not to understand.

To pull him down.

Their hands tore into the light, scattering stars like sparks in the dark. The sky collapsed inward. Yos fell—breath locked, heart hammering—

And he woke gasping, the darkness of his room rushing back as the echo of breaking light rang through his bones.

Foreshadowing Real Trouble

Yos woke to gray light filtering through the blinds.

For a moment, he didn't know where he was. The dream still clung to him—fractured sky, burning eyes, hands reaching through light. His chest felt tight, like he'd been running. He lay still, listening to the house breathe around him: pipes clicking awake, distant footsteps, the low murmur of a television downstairs.

Slowly, reality settled back in.

His room. His bed. The hoodie folded over the chair.

Yos sat up and pressed his palms into his eyes. The echo of the dream refused to fade. It wasn't fear exactly that lingered—it was certainty. A sense that something had shifted while he slept, that the fragile balance between them had cracked.

Downstairs, voices overlapped. Too sharp for a normal morning.

He pulled on the hoodie before he could overthink it and went to find out why.

The living room was half-lit, the curtains still drawn. The TV played on mute, flickering color across the walls. Dany sat on the edge of the couch, elbows on his knees, hands clasped so tightly his knuckles had gone pale.

He was staring at nothing.

"Dany?" Yos said.

Dany startled, jerking upright like he'd been caught doing something wrong. "Uh—yeah. Hey."

"You okay?" Yos asked, keeping his voice light.

"Yeah," Dany said too quickly. "Just thinking."

Dany had always been the kindest of the three. He noticed when people were hurting. He apologized even when things weren't his fault. But he was also the easiest to pull, caught in the gravity of stronger voices.

A follower—even when it hurt him.

Yos didn't move closer. He didn't push.

"You sure?" he asked gently.

Dany nodded, but his eyes gave him away. Guilt lived there, heavy and unsteady, like he was already apologizing for something he hadn't done yet.

"Things are tense," Dany admitted at last. His voice dropped. "Kamal's angry. Rafi's…Rafi." He swallowed. "They think Dad's ignoring us. Favoring you."

The words landed hard.

Yos felt his stomach drop. "I don't want that."

"I know," Dany said quickly. "I really do. But they don't see it that way."

He hesitated, fingers tightening together. The room seemed to hold its breath.

"They're planning something," Dany said quietly.

Yos froze.

"What kind of something?"

Dany shook his head. "I don't know. They won't tell me everything." His voice cracked just slightly. "But it's about you."

The silence that followed felt louder than shouting.

That evening, the house had the tense stillness of a storm waiting to break.

Yos moved through the hallway carefully, every step measured. As he passed Kamal's room, he heard voices—low, sharp, shaped into something dangerous by the narrow crack of the door.

He slowed.

Kamal's voice came first, tight with anger.

"He thinks he's better than us."

Rafi answered, calm and cutting.

"He doesn't have to think it. Dad already does."

Dany's voice slipped in, uncertain.

"Maybe we shouldn't—"

"Shut up, Dany," Kamal snapped. "You know I'm right."

Yos's pulse thundered in his ears.

Rafi spoke again, colder now. More deliberate.

"If people saw the real Yos, they'd finally stop worshipping him."

"Yeah," Kamal said. "We just need to show them."

There was a pause.

Dany whispered something Yos couldn't hear. The words were swallowed by the walls.

Rafi replied without hesitation.

"We're not hurting him. Just his image. That's enough."

Kamal let out a short, humourless laugh.

"Exactly. Let's knock him off his little pedestal."

Yos felt the floor tilt beneath him.

He stepped back before the door could creak, before his breath could betray him. His heart pounded so hard it felt visible, like it might echo down the hallway.

They were talking about him like he wasn't a person.

Like he was a problem to solve.

Yos turned slowly and walked away, each step careful, controlled. He didn't let himself run. He didn't let himself react.

Not yet.

The house felt different now—narrower, colder, like the walls had shifted inward.

He didn't breathe properly until he reached the stairwell.

Yos leaned against the banister, fingers gripping the wood, lungs finally dragging in air. His chest ached. The dream rose up in his mind uninvited—hands tearing at light, jealousy burning through familiar faces.

It hadn't been just a dream.

It had been a warning.

And now, wide awake, Yos understood what the stars had tried to show him:

The fall wouldn't come from strangers.

It would come from home.

Mara Again

Yos lay on his bed with the lights off, phone resting heavy in his hand. The house had gone quiet, but the silence wasn't peaceful—it pressed in, thick with things he now knew and couldn't unknow.

He stared at the screen longer than necessary before typing.

Yos: Are you awake?

The typing bubble appeared almost immediately. That alone eased something tight in his chest.

Mara: Yeah. What's wrong?

His thumbs hovered. How did you explain that the people who shared your blood were turning you into a target? That the place meant to be safest no longer felt that way?

He didn't try.

Yos: Can we talk tomorrow?

Three dots. Gone. Then back again.

Mara: Of course. Whatever it is, we'll figure it out.

Yos read the message twice. Then a third time.

We'll figure it out.

The words settled into him slowly, like warmth seeping through cold hands. His breathing evened without him noticing. For the first time since the dream, since the hallway, since the warning from Dany, the ground felt less likely to split beneath him.

He typed a reply, erased it, then settled on something simple.

Yos: Thanks.

Mara: Always.

He set the phone down and stared at the ceiling, the faint glow of passing headlights tracing soft lines above him. He wasn't used to we. His life had been a careful practice in handling things alone—being quiet enough, careful enough, small enough not to make waves.

But tonight, the idea of not being alone felt like an anchor.

And he needed it more than ever.

Yos pulled the hoodie closer around himself and turned onto his side. Somewhere down the hall, a door closed. Footsteps passed. Laughter—sharp, unfamiliar—cut through the quiet and then vanished.

Tomorrow loomed in his mind, heavy and undefined.

But Mara would be there.

He held onto that thought as sleep finally found him, fragile but real.

End of Set-Up: The Brothers' Plot

In the brothers' room, the decision was made.

The air felt stale, heavy with unspoken resentment. Clothes lay half-folded on the floor, a chair pushed back at an angle like it had been kicked aside earlier. The single overhead light buzzed faintly, casting sharp shadows that stretched and bent along the walls.

Kamal paced the length of the room like a caged animal, boots striking the floor in tight, angry steps. His hands curled and uncurled at his sides, energy coiled and looking for release.

"We're doing this," he said, voice low but absolute. "He needs to be put in his place."

The words weren't shouted. They didn't need to be. They carried the weight of a verdict already decided.

Rafi leaned back against the desk; one foot hooked around the leg of a chair. Where Kamal burned hot, Rafi was cool controlled. A smirk tugged at his mouth, his eyes glinting with sharp, deliberate interest.

"I've already got a plan," he said. "Something public."

He let the pause stretch, savouring it.

"Something he can't come back from."

Dany sat on the edge of the bed, shoulders rounded, fists clenched so tightly his knuckles had gone white. His chest felt tight, like guilt itself had taken physical shape inside him. He stared at the floor, at a loose thread on the carpet, anywhere but at his brothers' faces.

He didn't speak.

He didn't stop them.

And that silence echoed louder than any agreement.

Kamal stopped pacing and turned, the decision finally settling into his posture. He cracked his knuckles—once, twice—the sound sharp in the small room.

"Good," he said. "Let's ruin Yos's golden-boy reputation."

Rafi nodded, already pulling his phone from his pocket, thumbs moving as if the future were just another message waiting to be sent. "Starting tomorrow."

The light overhead flickered once.

Dany's throat burned. His hands loosened, then clenched again. He felt himself splitting—between loyalty and fear, between love and weakness.

So softly that neither of them heard, he whispered into the growing dark:

"I'm sorry, Yos…"

The apology hung in the room, unanswered, as the plan settled into place

Part II — The Shadows

(Betrayal and confinement)

I dreamed of glass walls

that shimmered when I breathed —

reflections of faces I couldn't reach.

Every time I touched the light,

it turned to dust in my hands.

(Symbol: Entrapment, loss of trust, illusions of truth.)

Catalyst

Yos had barely slept.

He carried the weight of last night's overheard whispers in the tightness of his chest and the heaviness of his steps. The halls of the school felt different today—thicker, like the air itself was bracing for something.

Students moved in clusters. Heads turned. Whispers fluttered behind cupped hands.

Yos kept walking, hoping he was imagining it.

He wasn't.

When he reached his locker, he found Mara already waiting. Her face was pale with worry.

"Yos," she said softly. "Something's happening."

He forced a small smile. "Yeah, I kind of felt that."

"No," she whispered urgently. "It's worse."

Before he could ask, three administrators rounded the corner—principal, vice principal, tech-security officer— moving with the grim certainty of people who believed they already knew the truth.

"Yosef Darai," the principal said. "Come with us."

Every conversation in the hall shrivelled into silence.

Mara reached for his arm. "I'll be right here. Okay?"

Yos nodded, even though nothing felt okay.

They ushered him into the conference room. Its cold white lights made everything feel clinical and merciless.

On the table lay a thick folder.

Another screen beside it displayed lines of code—lines he didn't recognize—along with transaction logs, flagged emails, and digital footprints stamped with his username.

The principal folded her hands. "We've received reports," she began, "and we've verified that someone using your credentials accessed restricted school servers last night."

The tech officer clicked a key. More data filled the screen, scrolling like a verdict already written.

"Hacking," she said.

"Unauthorized data extraction."

"Attempted financial fraud."

Yos blinked. The words didn't make sense. They were too sharp, too wrong.

"I—I didn't do any of that," he said quietly.

The vice principal leaned forward. "The evidence says otherwise."

"I don't even know how to hack anything."

"Your device was used," the tech officer replied. "Your account. Your ID."

Yos felt heat rising behind his eyes. "Someone set me up."

The principal sighed, the way adults sigh when they think a child is lying to protect himself. "Yosef, please. You need to be honest with us."

"I am being honest," Yos whispered.

They questioned him for half an hour.

Every word he said sounded smaller than the accusation.

Every explanation felt like it dissolved before reaching them.

They didn't want the truth—only closure.

Finally, the principal closed the folder with a soft, devastating finality. "Given the severity of the offense, and the verified digital trail," she said, "the school has no choice."

Her next words cut sharper than any dream ever could:

"You are expelled effective immediately."

The room tilted.

Yos sat frozen, unable to breathe, unable to understand how quickly his life had been rewritten.

His father's words echoed distantly—Dreams aren't for escaping life—they're for shaping it.

But this felt like life reshaping him without permission.

"I didn't do it," he said again, because it was the only truth he had left.

The vice principal looked away. The tech officer powered down the screen. The decision had already been made.

When they handed him the expulsion papers, his fingers trembled so violently he almost couldn't hold them.

The walk home was mute.

He didn't text Mara. He didn't take the bus. He didn't cry.

He felt hollow—like someone had scraped the meaning out of him and left an empty shape behind.

When he opened the apartment door, his father turned at the sound. He froze when he saw Yos's face, then saw the papers in his hands.

"What happened?" his father asked, voice already breaking.

Yos opened his mouth, but the words came out jagged. "Dad…I was expelled."

His father's breath hitched. "What? Why?"

"They think I hacked the school…stole data." Yos shook his head, voice cracking. "I didn't do it."

His father crossed the room in two strides, gripping Yos's shoulders. "Look at me. I know you didn't."

Something inside Yos crumpled at that—relief laced with grief.

"But they have…evidence," Yos whispered. "Fake data. Fake everything."

His father pulled him into a hug, one arm around his back, the other cradling the back of his head like he was a child again. Yos felt the tremor in his father's hands.

"Oh, my boy…" his father murmured. "My boy, I'm so sorry."

But the moment of comfort couldn't hide the truth.

His father stepped back, looking suddenly older, his eyes wet but burning. "I'll talk to them," he said. "I'll fix this. They can't do this to you."

Yos shook his head. "They already did."

"No," his father said fiercely. "No, I won't let them."

But even as he said it, Yos saw the doubt in his father's face—saw the way the injustice gnawed at him.

Saw the heartbreak.

Not just because the school had failed his son.

Because the world had failed the quiet, gentle boy he'd tried so hard to protect.

His father sank into a chair, hands covering his face. "This isn't right," he whispered. "You don't deserve this. You never deserved any of it."

Yos felt tears prick his eyes. He didn't want to cry in front of him, but the weight was too much.

"I don't understand," Yos said. "Why would someone do this to me?"

But he did understand.

Deep down, in a place he didn't want to admit existed, he knew exactly who had done it.

That night, Yos sat alone in his room, the expelled-student packet open on his lap. His hoodie felt heavier than usual, as though absorbing all his fear and shame.

His dreams were supposed to guide him.

But today had swallowed every trace of direction.

The world felt cruel in a way he had never allowed himself to believe before. His belief in fairness—his quiet faith that truth eventually rose—began to crack.

Maybe the world isn't listening, he thought.

Maybe truth doesn't speak loudly enough.

Outside his door, he heard the muffled voices of his brothers—one amused, one satisfied, one distressed.

And Yos realized something:

This wasn't an accident.

It wasn't random.

It wasn't fate.

It was betrayal.

And it was only the beginning.

Debate

Night folded itself around Yos like a dark, indifferent blanket.

He sat on the floor beside his bed, legs pulled to his chest, the expulsion papers spread around him like debris from a fallen building. His mind replayed the morning in loops— questions, accusations, disbelief. Every replay made the room feel smaller.

Hacking.

Fraud.

Expelled.

The words didn't attach to him. They felt like labels pasted on the wrong person. Someone louder. Someone reckless. Someone who didn't care.

Not him.

Not the quiet boy who wrote his dreams down like prayers.

His father knocked softly. "Yos? Can I come in?"

Yos wiped his eyes without answering. The door opened a crack anyway. His father peeked in, face lined with worry.

"Did you eat?" he asked.

Yos shook his head.

"I'll make something."

"Dad…I'm not hungry."

His father hesitated, then entered and sat beside him on the floor. They sat shoulder to shoulder, saying nothing. Silence, the kind Yos usually loved, pressed painfully against his ribs.

Finally, his father murmured, "We'll prove you're innocent. I know we will."

Yos closed his eyes. That faith, spoken so gently, hurt more than cruelty would have.

"But what if we can't?" Yos whispered.

His father rubbed a hand over his face. "Then the world is wrong. Not you."

Yos wanted to believe him.

But the world felt very big, and he felt very small.

After his father left, Yos crawled onto his bed and stared at the ceiling, mind churning.

Should he fight this?

He imagined storming into the school, demanding justice, shouting until they finally heard him. But the thought collapsed under its own weight. He wasn't built for shouting battles. His voice was made of softer things.

So, was he supposed to surrender?

Accept the lie?

Let the world stamp him with a story that wasn't his?

Neither option felt like survival.

His dreams used to guide him. But now even sleep felt treacherous.

He pressed his face into the hoodie sleeve and cried until the fabric clung damply to his cheek.

Morning came without permission.

His father was already gone off to argue with administrators, he'd said. Off to "fight this nonsense." Yos wished he hadn't gone. Not because he didn't want help—but because he didn't want to see his father fail.

He wandered the apartment like a ghost. The walls felt unfamiliar. The silence felt dangerous. His brothers avoided his eyes. Kamal kept his door shut. Rafi hummed as he buttered toast—an unsettling, satisfied little tune.

Dany, guilt wrapped around him like chains, approached timidly.

"Yos…" he began. "Are you okay?"

Yos blinked. "No."

Dany deflated. "I didn't know they'd push it this far. I thought…it was just a prank. Just humiliation. I never thought they'd—"

"Expel me?" Yos finished softly.

Dany flinched like he'd been hit. "I'm so sorry."

Yos swallowed. "I know."

Dany didn't deserve the truth Yos felt burning in his chest— you could've stopped them.

But he left that part unspoken.

The day dragged.

Should he try to clear his name?

Or accept that the world didn't care about truth?

He opened his journal, hoping for clarity, but the page stared back blankly, accusing him of losing the very thing that defined him.

His dreams.

His compass.

His belief in meaning.

"All broken," he muttered.

He slammed the journal shut.

When the doorbell rang, Yos didn't move. He wasn't expecting anyone.

But footsteps approached his room.

A moment later, his father called gently, "Yos? There's someone here to see you."

Yos frowned. "Who?"

"Recruiter," his father said, voice unreadable. "Something about a Youth Initiative…from a company called Orion Systems."

Yos sat up. "Orion Systems? Why would they—?"

"I don't know," his father said honestly. "But…maybe you should hear them out."

Yos hesitated. He didn't trust strangers, not when his world was already collapsing. But he followed his father to the living room anyway.

A woman stood near the couch—tall, crisp uniform, hair pulled tightly back. She carried a tablet under one arm.

She smiled professionally. "Yosef Darai? Thank you for meeting with me."

Yos nodded warily.

"I'm Recruiter Lang from Orion Systems' Youth Initiative Program," she said. "We scout young individuals with… unusual cognitive potential."

Yos blinked. "I think you have the wrong person."

Lang shook her head. "We've been monitoring academic performance, creative profiles, and behavioural markers. You're exactly the type of candidate we seek."

He stared. "But…why now?"

Lang hesitated just long enough for Yos to catch the truth.

"You've come onto our radar due to recent…digital irregularities."

Yos's stomach twisted. "You mean the hacking accusations?"

She nodded. "We reviewed the same data your school received."

His father stiffened. "Then you know it's false."

Lang's expression remained neutral. "We know it wasn't Yos performing the breach. But the event indicates something important: Yos has become an outlier."

"Outlier?" his father repeated.

"In ways we value," Lang said simply.

Yos's pulse quickened. He didn't understand. None of this made sense.

Lang continued, "When systems break around a person, we pay attention. Sometimes it's a sign of someone destined for unconventional paths."

Yos swallowed. "Are you saying this is…good?"

"I'm saying it's opportunity," she replied.

She extended a sleek brochure toward him—metallic blues, constellations, the Orion logo glowing faintly.

"This program takes students who've fallen through society's cracks," she said. "Gives them training, resources, mentorship. A new direction."

Direction.

The word hit him like a knock on the soul.

His father looked at him anxiously. "Yos…you don't have to decide anything right now."

But Lang stepped closer. "We believe your mind works differently. We can help you understand that difference. Shape it."

The word "shape" echoed his father's line from before—

Dreams aren't for escaping life—they're for shaping it.

Yos took the brochure.

His hands trembled slightly.

Images filled the pages—students learning advanced tech, exploring starlit observatories, training under mentors. A tagline read:

"Find where your mind belongs."

Belongs.

Yos felt something tighten painfully in his chest.

"I don't understand," he said quietly. "Why me?"

Lang studied him. "Because you still believe the world has meaning—even when it hurts you. People like you change things."

Yos's breath hitched. He wasn't sure if that was true. But the idea was intoxicating in a world that had just rejected him.

After Lang left, promising to return tomorrow for an answer, Yos collapsed onto the couch. His father sat beside him, hands folded tightly.

"You don't have to go," his father said. "We can fight this. Together."

"Fight how?" Yos whispered.

"We'll appeal. We'll hire someone. We'll—"

"Dad," Yos interrupted softly, "the school doesn't want to hear the truth."

His father's throat bobbed. "But I do."

Yos looked at him with burning eyes. "I know. But…it's not enough."

Silence held them.

Finally, his father put a hand on his shoulder. "If you go… promise me it's because you want a future. Not because you're running."

Yos nodded weakly. "I don't know what I want. I just know I can't stay here."

His father's eyes glistened. "You're still my son. Wherever you go."

That night, Yos sat by his window, hoodie wrapped tight around him. His restless thoughts were trying to find patterns.

Should he stay and fight?

Should he cling to the truth until the truth disappeared from everyone but him?

Or was this exile disguised as destiny?

His heart ached. "Tell me what to do," he whispered to no one.

The sky didn't answer.

But something inside him shifted—quietly, like a page turning.

He opened his journal.

For the first time since the expulsion, he wrote:

I don't know if justice exists the way I thought.

Maybe truth whispers too quietly for most people to hear.

But maybe quiet isn't weakness.

Maybe quiet is direction.

He paused, then added:

If the world won't give me space to exist, maybe I need to find new space.

Or make it.

He dreamed again.

The star-field returned—but this time, he didn't rise. The stars hovered around him, dimmer, uncertain.

Behind him, the shadows of his brothers lurked at the edge of the horizon, faceless and distant.

Ahead of him, a narrow path of starlight stretched into the dark—thin, trembling, but undeniably there.

He stepped onto it.

The stars brightened.

He woke with his decision quietly settled inside his chest.

At breakfast, he spoke before his courage vanished.

"Dad," he said softly, "I'm going."

His father lowered his coffee slowly, eyes tightening with pain—but also something else.

Acceptance.

"You're sure?" he asked.

Yos nodded. "I have to. I can't stay where people only see lies. Maybe…maybe Orion is where I figure out who I'm supposed to be."

His father exhaled shakily. "Then I'll support you. Even if it breaks my heart."

"It breaks mine too," Yos whispered.

They hugged tightly. For a long time.

His brothers watched silently from the hallway.

Kamal's face was unreadable.

Rafi's was cold with satisfaction.

Dany's was breaking apart piece by piece.

But none of them spoke.

Yos looked at them—really looked—and realized something painful:

He still loved them.

Even now.

Even after everything.

He lowered his eyes.

"Goodbye," he murmured.

None of them answered.

That afternoon, Recruiter Lang returned.

Yos stepped out of the apartment with his backpack slung over one shoulder, journal tucked safely inside, hoodie zipped up to his throat.

As the door closed behind him, he felt something shift.

A soft cracking inside his chest—

part grief, part fear, part hope—

the quiet shattering of innocence.

And the beginning of exile.

Break Into Two

The transport car waited at the curb like a sleek, silent predator. Black, windowless except for a narrow front slit, its surface reflected nothing—absorbing light instead of giving it back.

Recruiter Lang stood beside it, hands folded behind her back.

Yos stood on the apartment steps, backpack heavy on his shoulders, heart heavier still.

His father lingered inside the doorway, trying and failing to smile.

"You'll call?" his father asked.

"Every day," Yos promised, though he wasn't sure if Orion would allow it.

He hugged him again—tight, desperate, memorizing the warmth.

Then came the moment between moments: the soft click of letting go.

Yos stepped forward.

The world he knew stepped backward.

Lang opened the transport door.

"This way."

And just like that, Yos left home.

Inside, the transport was dim, lined with metallic panels that hummed with low energy. No seats—just molded benches. No windows—just a long, pulsing strip of white light tracing the ceiling.

The door sealed with a hiss.

Yos's chest tightened.

"Where are we going exactly?" he asked.

Lang didn't look at him. "Orion Systems Central Campus."

"What is it like?"

"Efficient."

The car vibrated, then glided forward with unnatural smoothness.

Yos clutched his backpack and breathed slowly. He imagined the dream—the quiet light, the understanding silence. He tried to hold onto it.

But the world outside blurred into nothing, and the hum of

the car erased the memory.

The transport emerged into blinding white brightness.

Yos blinked hard.

Orion Systems rose before him—an impossible skyline of glass and metal. Towers with edges too sharp for the human eye, walkways suspended with invisible supports, drones carving silent arcs through the air.

Everything was monochrome. Everything gleamed with sterilized perfection.

Lang stepped out first. "Welcome to Orion."

Yos followed reluctantly, boots touching the polished ground that reflected his shape but not his warmth.

People in identical uniforms strode across the plaza—no variation, no chatter, expressionless. Their movements were synchronized, as if the place itself dictated their cadence.

A cold wind swept through the corridors between buildings, carrying the faint scent of ozone.

"This way," Lang said.

Yos pulled his hoodie tighter. It was the only softness in sight.

They entered the main building—a towering monolith of glass that tinted the sky a sterile silver. Inside, the air felt recycled, filtered of impurities…including emotion.

Yos's footsteps echoed too clearly, as if the walls were empty.

Screens glowed everywhere, displaying meaningless data streams:

bar graphs flickering, neural diagrams rotating, slogans appearing and dissolving:

ORION: OPTIMIZATION IS HUMANITY'S FUTURE.

REMOVING THE ERRATIC. ENHANCING THE EFFICIENT.

Yos shivered.

"This place feels…" His voice trailed off.

"Controlled?" Lang supplied.

Yos nodded.

"That is the point."

He wasn't sure if she meant it as comfort.

Lang led him to a corridor lined with silver doors. Each one slid open silently when approached and sealed instantly after. No handles. No privacy.

"This is the training wing," she explained. "You'll be evaluated, assigned, and integrated here."

"What about…my schedule?" Yos asked.

"There is no personal schedule. All participants follow The Structure."

"What about free time?"

She blinked at him, confused. "Free…time? Orion does not operate on outdated concepts of unstructured idleness."

Yos's throat tightened.

"And dreams?" he asked before he could stop himself. "I mean—sleep? Rest?"

Lang paused at a biometric scanner and looked at him with a curious sort of detachment.

"We do not encourage subconscious interference. Dreams are inefficient—disruptive. You will receive regulated sleep cycles with neural dampeners."

"Dampeners?" Yos repeated, horrified.

"To prevent dreaming."

He stopped walking. "But dreams are—"

"Unnecessary," she said firmly. "And you will learn to live without them."

The hallway lights flickered. For a heartbeat, the air felt colder.

Yos touched his hoodie, grounding himself in the last

trace of home.

They entered a circular room with seats arranged in concentric patterns around a central platform. Screens wrapped the walls.

Other recruits sat silently, eyes forward, hands still.

No whispering.

No fidgeting.

No individuality.

A voice—calm, synthetic—filled the room:

"Welcome to Orion Systems' Youth Initiative. You are here because the world outside failed you, or you failed it. Here, there is no failure. Only correction."

Yos's stomach twisted.

"Emotion is distraction. Intuition is noise. Creativity is deviation. Here, you will become functional."

The words hit him like cold rain.

Functional.

Not inspired.

Not unique.

Not himself.

On the wall, an image of a brain diagram lit up—sections labeled "UNPRODUCTIVE" in red.

He felt sick.

As the presentation droned on, Yos scanned the room. The other recruits sat with hollow faces—obedient or afraid, he couldn't tell which.

He wondered if they had been broken first, like he had.

If they had been pushed into exile too.

He whispered under his breath, "What am I doing here?"

The recruit beside him didn't react. No one reacted.

Dreams weren't allowed here.

Meaning wasn't allowed here.

Even silence wasn't the kind he loved—this silence was suffocating, not listening.

His heartbeat thudded in his ears.

Was this destiny?

Or just another trap disguised as opportunity?

His father's voice drifted through his mind:

Dreams aren't for escaping life—they're for shaping it.

But Orion wanted to erase dreams entirely.

Was he supposed to let them?

After orientation, Lang guided him to his assigned room.

It was a white cube—nothing more.

A bed, a desk, a screen.

No colour. No warmth. No window.

On the wall, instructions flashed:

RULE 1: EMOTION IS IRRELEVANT.

RULE 2: INDIVIDUALITY IS INEFFICIENT.

RULE 3: DREAMING IS PROHIBITED.

Yos felt a crushing ache in his chest.

This was the new world.

These were the new rules.

He sat on the edge of the bed. The mattress felt synthetic, unyielding. Even the air felt hostile to softness.

He pulled the hoodie tighter around himself—the last piece of identity he had left.

The only thing Orion didn't strip away.

Yet.

Lang handed him a small silver device. "Your ID module."

Yos turned it over in his hands. No buttons. No ports. Just a flat slab of cold metal.

"It will monitor your biometric cycles, regulate your sleep, track your performance, and ensure compliance."

"Compliance?" Yos echoed.

Lang nodded. "Resistance is unnecessary and inefficient."

"What if I don't…fit?" he dared to ask.

She studied him for a long moment.

Not unkindly—just analytically.

"You didn't fit in your old world either."

The words hit too close.

Then she added, "But here, fitting isn't required. Obedience is."

She left him with that.

The door slid shut.

Yos was alone in a room that felt like it had never held a real person.

Yos sat on the bed, ID module clenched in his hands, hoodie wrapped around him like armour.

He thought of his father's hug.

Of Mara's encouragement.

Of his brothers' shadows in his dream.

He thought of the star-path.

Had he taken a wrong step?

Was this exile punishment…or preparation?

A low hum vibrated through the walls—machines breathing, systems thinking, Orion watching.

He felt impossibly small.

But inside the shrinking, something stirred.

A spark.

A tiny ember of defiance.

A truth he couldn't erase:

Dreams mattered.

Meaning mattered.

He mattered.

Even here.

Maybe especially here.

Yos lay back on the sterile bed, staring at the smooth ceiling.

"We do not encourage subconscious interference,"
Lang had said.

But Yos closed his eyes anyway.

He whispered to the darkness,

"I won't let you take my dreams."

For the first time since arriving, he didn't feel completely powerless.

Just exiled.

But not extinguished.

And exile, he realized, was not the end—

It was the beginning of a path no one at Orion could predict.

A new world had swallowed him.

But it had no idea what he carried inside.

Act II began with a quiet boy in a soulless facility…

and a dream the system could not control.

B Story

Mara: the one connection Yos didn't expect to find here.

Yos was halfway through his first "Cognitive Calibration Session" when the screen in front of him flickered.

Not a glitch — Orion didn't glitch.

Then a small text box appeared in the corner:

hello, dreamboy.

Yos's pulse jumped.

Only one person had ever called him that.

"Mara?" he whispered.

The screen flickered again — a soft ripple like laughter hiding in static.

don't talk. they monitor audio.

just watch.

The lesson resumed as if nothing had happened, but Yos's breath came faster.

Mara was here.

Not just here — inside the system.

And somehow, despite Orion's rules, she had found him first.

Later that day, during a supervised transit to another wing, a figure joined his group — same uniform, same blank expression as every other recruit.

But the eyes…

He recognized them instantly.

Mara.

Slightly older looking from stress, sharper around the edges, but undeniably her.

She didn't greet him.

Didn't smile.

Didn't break the robotic pace.

Not until the group turned a corner and the camera blinked into recalibration mode.

Then—only for a single second—she met his gaze and whispered:

"You shouldn't have come here."

Her voice wasn't angry.

It was scared.

Before he could speak, she stepped away and hardened her expression again.

Yos felt a sudden ache: relief, confusion, longing — all crashing together.

Over the next days, he saw her everywhere — passing through corridors, in training rooms, in cafeteria lines — but she always acted like she didn't know him.

Except for the coded messages.

They appeared on screens, in exam results, in system diagnostics:

stop smiling.

it draws attention.

don't trust orientation.

everything is recorded.

And sometimes, hidden deeper:

are you holding up?

…i'm trying.

Yos responded the only way he could: by keeping his head down, learning the systems, blending in.

But inside, the quiet warmth her presence sparked kept him breathing.

Three days in, during a mandatory "Sensory Recalibration Session," the lights cut out for two seconds — not a glitch, but a scheduled cycle.

In the darkness, Mara's whisper slid through the space between them:

"You're too hopeful for this place."

Yos turned. "Hope isn't a weakness."

"Here it is."

When the lights came back on, she was already looking straight ahead again, face blank.

But her words echoed through him.

She thought hope was dangerous.

He thought it was necessary.

Their truths collided quietly in the sterile air.

During a supervised walk back to quarters, Yos risked a whisper when they passed a blind corridor angle.

"You don't look happy here," he murmured.

Mara didn't slow, didn't look at him, but her voice was thin, almost brittle:

"Happiness isn't part of the program."

"But you used to believe in—"

"Don't," she cut in softly. "I don't believe in that anymore."

Something in her tone chilled him.

She wasn't angry.

She was tired.

Exhausted in a way that felt years older than her body.

He wanted to reach for her hand.

Instead, he stayed silent.

That night, a new message appeared on his screen:

check system folder x-17.

line 302.

He opened it carefully.

There, hidden inside Orion's sterile code, he found something impossible:

A poem.

Short, jagged, aching:

the machines think they erased me

but ghosts haunt circuits too

and i refuse to disappear

without leaving a scar

Yos covered his mouth, heart pounding.

She hadn't lost herself.

Not fully.

She hid rebellion in the only place Orion wasn't looking:

inside their own code.

Mara was still Mara.

Just buried.

The next morning, when they crossed paths in the Resource Hall, Yos murmured:

"I read it."

Mara froze — just for a heartbeat.

"You're going to get yourself flagged," she hissed under her breath.

"It was beautiful."

"Stop. Don't say things like that."

"Why?"

"Because beauty is inefficient."

"But you need it," Yos said softly. "Or you wouldn't be writing it."

Her jaw tightened.

For the first time, Yos saw not cynicism —

but fear.

As if hope was something she couldn't afford to touch.

Later, during neural-logic drills, another message flashed briefly across his data sheet:

hope doesn't save you.

it blinds you.

Yos pressed a hand to his chest.

He whispered, "It saved me once."

when?

the screen flickered.

"When I had no one else."

i'm not your hope.

stop looking at me like i am.

His heart tightened.

but i'm glad you're alive.

the final line read.

Then the message erased itself.

They sat across the cafeteria, far apart but facing each other.

Neither smiled. Neither spoke.

But their eyes met over identical trays of tasteless rations.

In her stare, he saw:

anger

fear

loneliness

and a spark — tiny, stubborn — she was trying to smother.

In his, she saw:

belief

gentleness

quiet fire.

Opposites.

But drawn across the sterile void between them.

A supervisor passed by, and they both looked down immediately.

But the connection stayed.

That night, a message appeared:

meet in corridor 6-F at 01:00.

cameras loop for 90 seconds.

don't be late.

Yos's stomach flipped.

He waited until the facility entered "Rest Cycle," then slipped out of his room, pulse hammering.

Mara was already there, leaning against the wall.

"Why did you call me?" Yos whispered.

She exhaled shakily. "Because I needed to remember what it feels like…to talk like a human."

Her voice trembled on the last word.

Yos felt something in his chest crack open.

They spoke in whispers:

"How long have you been here?" Yos asked.

"Six months."

"Why?"

"They found something in my aptitude scores."

She looked away. "Something they wanted to claim."

"What about your family?"

"They think I'm at a scholarship boarding school."

"And you let them believe that?"

Mara's eyes darkened. "Wouldn't you? They can't pull me out. Orion recruits don't get to leave."

Yos's stomach dropped.

He hadn't known that.

Mara saw the fear flicker in his expression and softened.

"Then again," she whispered, "you always were too honest to lie to the people you love."

"You shouldn't be here," Mara said. "You're…too soft for them."

"I'm stronger than I look."

"That's not what I mean."

She stepped closer.

"You're still dreaming. Even now. I can see it. In your eyes."

Yos looked down, embarrassed.

"Dreamers break here," she continued. "Orion doesn't crush people like me — we already cracked before we arrived. But you? You come in whole. They'll take that from you."

"I won't let them," Yos said quietly.

Mara gave a sad smile. "That's what scares me."

For 90 borrowed seconds, the world softened.

They whispered about the past —

school lunches

inside jokes

the rooftop where Yos used to write dreams

the quiet sanctuary they once shared.

Mara didn't laugh, but her eyes warmed.

"You always believed everything mattered," she murmured. "That every moment meant something."

"It does," Yos insisted gently.

"There's no meaning here, Yos."

He shook his head. "Then we make it."

Her breath caught.

She looked away too quickly.

Their connection — fragile, vulnerable — pulsed like a living thing between them.

Before they parted, Mara pressed a small data chip into his hand.

"What's this?" Yos whispered.

"A map," she said. "Not of the facility. Of me."

He stared, surprised.

"I hide pieces of myself in Orion's systems," she explained. "Memories. Poems. Feelings. If they scan my brain hard enough, they'll erase them. So I store them in code."

"Why give this to me?"

"Because…" She swallowed. "Because I don't trust anyone else to keep me alive."

Yos felt his chest expand painfully.

"I'll keep you alive," he promised.

Mara flinched as if he'd touched a bruise.

"Don't make promises you can't keep."

But she didn't take the chip back.

As the cameras began to unloop, she stepped back.

"Listen to me," she whispered. "There are things happening in Orion you don't understand. If you push too hard, they'll take your mind apart. Piece by piece."

"But you're fighting them," Yos said.

"I'm surviving them."

Her eyes softened. "And I…want you to survive too."

"Mara—"

"No."

Her voice cracked. "Don't make me hope again."

The lights brightened.

The cycle ended.

They stepped apart with mechanical precision, as if they'd never spoken at all.

But Yos's heart was burning.

Back in his room, Yos lay awake holding the chip.

A map of Mara.

A piece of her soul disguised as code.

He placed it under his pillow like a talisman.

Mara wasn't just a friend.

She wasn't just a link to home.

She was the reason this place didn't swallow him whole.

Her poetry — fragments of rebellion — inspired him.

Her cynicism challenged him.

Her presence grounded him.

Together, they sparked something Orion couldn't regulate:

Humanity.

Training changed after that.

Yos didn't drift numbly through lessons anymore.

He watched for hidden layers.

Signals.

Flashes of subtext.

Mara had taught him that code wasn't always literal.

Sometimes it was a whisper.

A plea.

A wound.

He began seeing small clues everywhere — tiny anomalies in the system.

Mara's fingerprints, subtle but defiant.

He wondered how long she'd been fighting alone.

He wondered if she'd let him fight with her.

Days passed.

They rarely spoke.

But they communicated.

A stray line of altered code.

A shifted data packet.

A glitch only the two of them noticed.

Each message said:

I'm here.

You're not alone.

We remain human.

Yos felt stronger.

Braver.

More certain that he hadn't made a mistake by coming.

If Orion was a machine, he and Mara were the gears refusing to fall in line.

During a group evaluation, a line of text flickered briefly on his personal screen:

do you still believe dreams shape life?

Yos typed an answer quickly, knowing the system would erase it:

yes.

She responded:

then prove it.

The words hit him hard.

She wasn't mocking him.

She was testing him.

Inviting him.

Challenging him to hold onto something she'd already lost.

One evening, during supervised recreation, Mara brushed past him.

Her hand didn't touch his — but it came close enough to feel the heat of her skin.

"Don't let Orion change you," she whispered.

"Even if I already let it change me."

Yos looked at her. Really looked.

Her cynicism wasn't cruelty.

It was armour.

Worn down by months in this place.

He wanted to give her back the hope she'd lost.

But for now, he simply said:

"I won't let them take either of us."

For the first time, she didn't argue.

Late that night, Yos found a new message hidden in his diagnostics file.

Just three words:

keep dreaming, yos.

He touched the screen gently.

Mara didn't believe in dreams anymore.

But she believed in him.

And in Orion's mechanical world, that was the most dangerous — and beautiful — rebellion of all.

Fun and Games

By the third week, Yos understood one thing:

Orion ran everything on patterns.

Patterns inside patterns.

Loops wrapped in logic.

Systems that looked flawless — until you looked closely.

That was where he excelled.

Not in algorithms.

Not in protocols.

But in intuition — the same strange instinct that shaped his dreams.

He didn't read code.

He *listened* to it.

To the way it pulsed.

To the way it breathed.

Because everything breathed here.

Even the machines.

During a diagnostic exam, each recruit had to identify a corrupted sequence.

Others stared blankly at their screens.

Orion designed these tests to be impossible at early levels.

But Yos closed his eyes.

He slowed his breath.

He imagined the code not as strings of characters —

but as a string of light, humming, moving, shifting.

When he opened his eyes, he saw it:

A single line—

seemingly perfect—

but pulsing wrong, like a silent scream.

He tapped the key.

Sequence isolated.

Error corrected.

The instructor blinked.

"This level isn't meant to be solvable at your stage."

Yos shrugged. "Maybe the stage is wrong."

Mara smiled at him from across the room—

small, proud, and quickly hidden.

People noticed.

Recruits whispered about the boy who "saw things."

The one who solved tests in seconds.

Who answered questions before they fully formed.

Who moved through the sterile halls with quiet certainty.

They called him the Listener.

A joke at first.

But the name stuck.

And Yos found that the more he listened — truly listened — the more the system revealed.

Sometimes it was a flicker in the lights.

Sometimes a glitch that shouldn't exist.

Sometimes a word hidden in the static.

He found echoes in the machine.

Whispers of individuality.

Ghosts of forgotten emotion.

It felt almost mystical.

Yos didn't try to inspire anyone.

He didn't lecture.

He didn't rebel openly.

But when he dared to smile in the cafeteria, three others tried too.

When he looked supervisors in the eye instead of the floor, others raised their chins.

When he whispered a gentle "It's okay" to a trembling first-year, the boy breathed easier the rest of the day.

Mara watched all of this with a mix of wonder and fear.

"You're going to get in trouble," she murmured.

"Why?"

"Because you make people feel human. Orion hates that."

Yos smiled. "Then they should've made their machines better."

She fought a smile — and lost.

One afternoon, in the Observation Wing, a woman in silver and white paused outside Yos's orientation room.

Tall.

Elegant.

Eyes sharp as glass.

Mara stiffened beside him.

"Don't look at her," she whispered. "That's Selene Porter."

"The CEO's wife," Yos whispered back.

"No," Mara corrected. "The real power."

Selene watched the recruits like she was studying rare insects.

Her gaze landed on Yos.

He felt it — a cold, clinical curiosity.

She turned to a technician.

"That one," she said. "The quiet one. Pull his long-term patterns."

Yos shivered.

Selene smiled faintly at his reaction —

as if she liked the fear.

Then she walked away.

That night, Yos dreamed.

He stood inside a glass tower—

smooth, gleaming, endless.

The walls reflected nothing.

The ceiling mirrored the ground.

He was trapped inside pieces of himself.

Then—

A crack.

Thin at first.

A hairline fracture darting like lightning.

Then another.

And another.

The entire tower shivered.

He held his breath.

The structure groaned, then split.

Light spilled in from somewhere unseen —

wild, burning, holy.

He reached for it.

The dream shattered.

Yos woke sweating.

Mara found him pale the next morning.

"You look like you saw a ghost," she whispered.

"I saw a tower," he murmured. "A perfect one. Cracking."

Mara's eyes widened slightly.

"That's…not good."

"What does it mean?"

She looked away.

Her voice barely audible:

"Orion only breaks when something inside it refuses to die."

Yos swallowed.

"Then something's going to break," he said softly.

Mara didn't disagree.

Orion's new challenge arrived the next day:

a virtual labyrinth designed to test "mentally compliant navigation."

Recruits entered alone.

Most never finished.

The maze wasn't meant to be solved — it was meant to break spirit.

Yos stepped into the chamber.

The walls glowed with blue lines.

The floor hummed.

He waited.

The maze reshaped itself — walls shifting like ribs, doors opening and closing like eyes blinking.

Yos closed his eyes.

Listened.

There it was—

a faint heartbeat.

A rhythm in the pattern.

He followed it.

Turn after turn.

Pulse after pulse.

He walked the labyrinth like it was a dream he'd already lived.

When he reached the exit, the system froze.

Then printed:

UNEXPECTED OUTCOME.

MAZE COMPLETED.

Selene Porter appeared in the observation deck during his debrief.

Her heels clicked softly.

Her expression unreadable.

She studied Yos —

tilted her head —

leaned closer to the glass.

"He's different," she murmured to the technician.

"Ma'am, all recruits vary—"

"No," she said sharply. "This one *anticipates* the system."

He felt her eyes on him like cold fingertips.

Then she spoke directly into the intercom.

"Yos Darai."

His breath stopped.

"You are full of contradictions," she said. "I'm still deciding if that makes you valuable…"

A pause.

"Or dangerous."

The intercom clicked off.

Mara grabbed his wrist afterward.

"Stay away from her," she whispered. "Selene doesn't admire people. She consumes them."

After the maze test, even supervisors whispered.

The boy who solved the impossible.

The Listener.

The Dreamer.

The one whose intuition outpaced math.

Small rebellions increased across the centre:

Someone hummed in the hall.

Someone joked about lunch flavour.

Someone added colour to their report signature.

Tiny sparks.

Tiny breaths of humanity.

And all of them traced back to Yos.

Not because he tried to lead them.

But because people wanted to follow a light in the dark.

Mara pulled him aside in a dead corridor.

"You need to stop."

"Stop what?"

"Being…you."

He blinked.

"Yos, you don't understand. This place doesn't tolerate anomalies. You survive by shrinking. By becoming predictable."

"I'm not trying to stand out—"

"But you do," she whispered fiercely. "And they're watching."

Her hands trembled.

"Please. If you die here, it will break me."

Yos's heart twisted.

He placed a gentle hand over hers.

"I won't die," he said softly. "I promise."

She closed her eyes.

"You shouldn't make promises you can't keep."

During group silence periods, Yos tapped patterns on the desk — soft rhythmic beats.

Others copied him.

Like heartbeat signals.

Like reminders that they were alive.

Supervisors ignored it at first.

Then frowned.

Then tried to isolate the source.

But the pattern kept moving.

Spreading.

A quiet rebellion in plain sight.

Mara watched, a fragile smile ghosting across her lips.

"You're ridiculous," she whispered.

"Why?"

"You're turning Orion into a drum circle."

Yos grinned.

"Better than a morgue."

Yos spent nights studying the chip Mara gave him —

the one containing pieces of her soul.

Memories encoded as strings.

Poems hidden like contraband.

Fragments of childhood laughter represented by binary rhythms.

It felt sacred.

He began adding to it —

quiet lines of empathy,

small reflections,

soft codes of hope.

He hid his contributions deep inside —

never overwriting hers.

When he handed the chip back, she looked at him with startled eyes.

"You added to it?"

"Only where you left space."

She swallowed hard.

"That's…

the kindest thing anyone's done for me."

Selene Porter began appearing more often.

Sometimes on upper walkways.

Sometimes behind glass.

Sometimes on silent screens.

Always watching.

Never smiling.

Mara noticed before Yos did.

"She's studying you."

"Why?"

"Because she sees something she can't categorize. Something she can't map."

"And that scares her?"

"No," Mara said darkly. "It fascinates her."

Yos felt a chill crawl up his spine.

Another dream.

He stood in the glass tower again —

but this time, people were inside with him.

Nameless recruits.

Machines.

Supervisors.

Mara.

All trapped.

The cracks spread like roots beneath their feet.

A loud, trembling hum filled the space —

the sound of something enormous straining to hold itself together.

Light poured through fractures.

Blinding.

Pure.

Something whispered:

"Break it."

He woke gasping.

This dream felt like more than a dream.

Like a prophecy.

"Mara," Yos said breathlessly at breakfast, "the tower cracked again. And light came through—"

"Stop," she hissed. "Don't speak about dreams here."

"But they mean something."

"Everything means something," she whispered, "but Orion punishes people who admit it."

She looked around nervously.

"What did the light look like?" she asked quietly.

He told her.

She pressed her lips together.

"Yos…that tower? It's real."

He blinked.

"What?"

"Not literally," she whispered. "But symbolically. Orion's entire hierarchy is built like a tower. Selene sits near the top."

"So, the dream means—"

"That she's cracking," Mara whispered.

Or the system itself was.

Selene Porter summoned him.

Not an invitation.

A demand.

Yos sat in a pristine white office, cold air brushing his neck.

Selene circled him slowly, like a curator examining an artifact.

"You navigate patterns differently," she said. "Your mind doesn't follow the usual linear structure."

"I just…listen."

"To what?"

He hesitated.

"To what feels true."

Selene smiled thinly.

"Truth is inefficient. But your intuition may be useful."

Her fingers hovered a breath above his cheek, not touching — assessing.

A shiver ran through him.

"You could rise high here, Yos Darai," she murmured. "If you stop pretending you have a choice."

He didn't answer.

She liked that.

When Yos returned, Mara dragged him into a supply alcove.

"What did she want?"

"To study me."

"Of course she did."

Mara's voice was brittle. "She collects things."

"I'm not a thing."

"She doesn't care."

Her breath shook.

"Yos…don't let her get inside your head. Once she's in, she never leaves."

Her fear wasn't jealousy in the romantic sense —

it was fear of losing him to the machine.

Fear of losing her last connection to herself.

Yos's influence grew in ways he didn't intend.

Recruits began leaving tiny marks of individuality:

Colored dots under collars.

Micro-graffiti in datapackets.

Shared glances.

Soft nods of solidarity.

Mara called it "the dream infection."

He called it humanity.

Even supervisors felt the shift —

the air buzzed with something unregulated.

Selene smiled more often when she passed.

Which terrified Mara.

"She likes disruption," Mara whispered. "Not because she wants change — but because she wants to own it."

"And she thinks she can own me?"

"Yes," Mara said. "And she's wrong. And that makes her

dangerous."

One day, the lights above Yos flickered in a
strange pattern —

not glitchy, but rhythmic.

Three pulses.

Pause.

Two pulses.

A code.

He whispered, "Who's sending this?"

The lights pulsed again.

Mara stared at the ceiling, stunned.

"That's not me," she said. "Or a recruit."

"Then who—?"

They looked at each other.

For the first time, Mara said it aloud:

"Something inside Orion is waking up."

During a neural-sync test, Yos felt the machine reading him.

Probing.

Mapping.

He slowed his breath.

Listened inside himself.

Listened to the machine.

Listened to the silence between both.

And for the briefest moment—

he felt something ancient.

Something waiting.

A presence inside Orion.

Not human.

Not machine.

Something in-between.

Something that recognized him.

He jerked back, gasping.

The supervisor frowned. "Yos? Are you malfunctioning?"

"No," he whispered. "Just…listening."

Mara found him trembling afterward.

"What happened?"

"There's something in the system," he said. "It noticed me."

Mara's face went pale.

"That's not possible."

"It spoke."

"What did it say?"

"That it knows me."

Mara grabbed his shoulders.

"Yos, you're not dealing with a ghost. You're dealing with Orion. The system is alive in ways you don't understand."

He swallowed.

"Maybe I'm supposed to."

"Don't say that" she begged.

But Yos didn't retract it.

When Yos returned to his room, he found something on his pillow:

A single shard of glass.

Clear.

Sharp.

Just like the tower in his dreams.

He touched it carefully.

It hummed.

Like it had a heartbeat.

Like it was a message.

He whispered, "What do you want from me?"

The shard pulsed once.

The dream came quickly that night.

He stood outside the glass tower this time.

Mara beside him.

Selene above, looking down from a balcony.

The cracks grew rapidly, crawling upward.

Inside the light, Yos saw—

The silhouettes of recruits.

Lost children.

Fragments of himself.

The tower groaned.

He felt the truth:

The tower was going to fall.

And he was part of the reason.

He woke with his heart shaking.

They met in a blind corner.

"Mara, the tower fell this time."

She inhaled sharply.

"That means collapse."

"Of Orion?"

"Of everything built on lies," she whispered.

He touched the shard he'd hidden in his sleeve.

"It left me…something."

Mara's eyes widened.

"You're attracting patterns that shouldn't exist."

"Maybe they're calling for help."

"Or maybe," she said darkly, "they're calling for destruction."

During a group assembly, when everyone stood silently, Yos raised one hand.

Not high — just slightly.

Someone else raised theirs.

Then another.

And another.

A wave of small gestures —

human, quiet, defiant —

moved through the recruits.

Not enough to alert supervisors.

But enough to say:

We're alive.

We're still here.

Mara watched with wide eyes.

She mouthed:

you're dangerous.

Yos mouthed back:

so are you.

Selene approached him after assembly.

"You create waves," she said softly. "Tiny ones. But enough to change currents."

"I'm not trying to change anything."

"I don't believe you."

Her smile was slow, clinical.

"You dream, don't you?"

Yos froze.

"No," he lied.

Selene leaned close.

"You forget…I married a man who lies for a living. Your eyes betray you."

His pulse hammered.

"We'll speak again soon," she murmured.

Mara grabbed his wrist afterwards, furious.

"Don't ever lie to her," she hissed. "She'll know. And she'll punish you for it."

The system itself began reacting to him.

Doors hesitated before sealing.

Lights flickered in patterns that followed him down halls.

Diagnostic programs glitched when he walked near them.

Recruits noticed.

Some whispered that Orion feared him.

Others whispered it wanted him.

Mara whispered:

"It's choosing you."

He whispered back:

"I didn't ask to be chosen."

She squeezed his hand.

"No one ever does."

One evening, they sat back-to-back in a hidden corner, shoulders touching.

"You're changing," Mara whispered. "Inside."

"So are you."

She exhaled painfully.

"I'm…starting to feel things again. And that terrifies me."

"Why?"

"Because feelings make you vulnerable."

"And strong," Yos whispered.

She didn't argue.

For a moment, the world felt warm again —

two sparks in a cold machine.

As Yos walked down the main corridor, he stopped abruptly.

The glass wall before him —

smooth, polished, perfect —

suddenly cracked.

Not physically.

Just for him.

A vision overlay.

A warning.

The same pattern from his dream.

He touched the glass.

The crack pulsed softly.

A whisper —

not heard, but felt:

Soon.

Yos shivered.

The tower was cracking in reality.

Mara found him whispering to the glass.

"What happened?"

"It cracked."

"There's no crack, Yos."

"Not for you."

She gripped his arms.

"You're seeing things that shouldn't exist. And Orion is reacting. This…this is bigger than us."

Yos swallowed hard.

"Then we'll face it together."

Mara looked at him like he was sunlight she couldn't bear to touch.

"You're impossible," she whispered.

He smiled softly.

"Impossible things are worth fighting for."

And as the lights dimmed for rest cycle,

a rumble echoed deep within the walls.

A warning.

A promise.

A machine beginning to fracture.

Midpoint

Yos was escorted by two silent guards to the highest restricted floor he had ever seen.

It felt familiar in a way that made his skin crawl—

smooth glass

white light

endless reflections.

The tower from my dreams, he thought.

The elevator opened into a circular chamber where Selene Porter waited alone.

She stood in a pale dress that glowed like liquid frost, hands clasped gently, expression unreadable.

"Yos," she said, almost warmly. "I've been expecting you."

Behind her, a panoramic glass wall revealed the entire Orion campus—lights humming in unison, people moving like programmed constellations.

The view was intoxicating.

The power in it was…undeniable.

"Do you know why I brought you here?" Selene asked.

Yos shook his head.

She stepped closer, her voice soft as silk and sharp as wire.

"You see patterns I've spent a lifetime trying to understand. You hear what others cannot. Orion needs that."

The glass behind her shifted data flowing up like waterfalls, global feeds merging and shimmering.

"With your intuition," she said, "we could shape a future beyond chaos. A world without unpredictability. Without suffering. Imagine an algorithm guided by your dreams—your instincts."

Yos's breath caught.

"You want to…use my dreams?"

"No," she corrected. "I want you to help me *run* the future."

His pulse hammered.

This was the offer people fantasized about.

Power. Purpose. Recognition.

A chance to belong.

A false victory wrapped in silver.

Selene extended her hand.

"You've lived in uncertainty all your life. People misunderstood you. Feared you. But here, Yos, you could be more than someone who listens to dreams. You could be someone who *defines* reality."

She gestured to the glass wall.

"In one year, you could command this facility. In two, entire networks. In five…"

Her voice dropped to a whisper.

"…the world."

Yos stared below.

For a moment, he felt the seductive pull of it—

the elegance

the symmetry

the power to shape something lasting

something clean

something certain.

A world where dreams weren't ridiculed.

Where he wasn't an outcast.

Where his differences weren't burdens but tools.

For one heartbeat, he imagined taking her hand.

The room flickered.

For a moment, he saw a hallucination—

or a warning.

Himself standing where Selene stood.

Recruits kneeling.

Lights pulsing under his command.

Machines echoing his thoughts.

He saw a future where he ruled the glass tower.

Where his dreams wrote the laws of reality.

Where truth bent to him.

It was intoxicating.

It was horrifying.

His fingers shook.

No.

Not this.

Dreams don't belong in cages.

Not mine.

Not anyone's.

He stepped back from Selene's outstretched hand.

"No."

Her smile froze.

Slowly, it dissolved.

"No?" she repeated softly, like she didn't understand the word.

"I won't use my dreams to control people."

"You misunderstand," she said. "You wouldn't control them. The algorithm would."

"That's worse," Yos whispered.

Her gaze sharpened.

"Truth doesn't need owners," he said. "And dreams…are meant to be free."

Selene studied him with chilling calm.

"You refuse power?"

"I refuse a prison shaped like power."

Silence cut the air.

Then Selene's expression darkened—

a storm rolling in.

"You disappoint me," she said quietly.

She walked back toward the glass wall, tapping her nails against it.

"You dreamers always pretend you want to save the world. But when offered the chance, you run."

"I'm not running."

"You are," she whispered, turning.

"Into naïve idealism."

Her eyes glittered.

"You could have ruled beside me. Together we could have shaped order from chaos. Now…"

She gestured to the guards.

"…you will be corrected."

Yos swallowed hard.

Selene stepped closer, lowering her voice to a venomous whisper.

"I offered you the future. You chose irrelevance."

Selene pressed a button on her wristband.

A holographic display appeared—

Yos's file

his tests

his "anomalies"

his dream patterns

his relationships

his messages

even hidden ones.

Mara's poems.

The rebellion seeds.

Every spark of humanity he'd spread.

All exposed.

Selene tapped a segment.

"Influence maps," she said.

"Do you know how many recruits have deviated from protocol because of you?"

Yos's stomach dropped.

Selene leaned in, voice soft as poison.

"You are destabilizing my system. And I do not tolerate instability."

For the first time, Yos lifted his chin toward her.

"Maybe your system needs destabilizing."

Selene froze.

For a moment, just a moment, he saw something flicker behind her eyes—

fear?

rage?

recognition?

None of it lasted.

"You're a child playing with matches," she whispered.

"Maybe," he said, "but fire brings light."

Her expression hardened.

"You brought this on yourself."

Selene snapped her fingers.

The lights in the room cut out.

The floor vibrated.

Security drones materialized from the walls.

A neural clamp unit descended from the ceiling.

Yos stepped back, heart racing.

"What are you doing?" he demanded.

"Retaliating," Selene said simply.

Two guards seized his arms.

Selene approached with slow, deliberate steps.

"You rejected my offer," she said. "So I will reshape you the hard way."

She raised the neural clamp.

"This will remove your impulses to dream. Permanently."

Yos struggled.

"Selene—don't—"

She touched his cheek with a cold fingertip.

"You wanted freedom.

I will give you silence instead."

As the clamp activated, Yos felt his mind break open.

A blinding flash.

A roaring silence.

A wave of light flooding his vision.

He saw—

The glass tower again.

But this time, it wasn't cracking.

It was exploding.

Shards flew outward like falling stars.

Light poured through every fragment.

Voices cried out—human voices, not machine signals.

And over it all, one whisper:

"Fight back."

He gasped.

The clamp flickered.

Sparks flew.

Selene's eyes widened.

"Impossible," she mouthed.

Yos collapsed to his knees as the clamp short-circuited.

The lights stuttered, pulsed, then stabilized.

Selene stared at the smoking device, stunned.

"You…broke it," she whispered.

"Your mind resisted a full neural override."

The guards pulled back, uncertain.

Selene's voice dropped to a terrifying calm.

"This changes everything."

Her eyes gleamed with a new hunger.

Not admiration.

Not even anger.

Possession.

"You are no longer a recruit, Yos Darai."

She stepped toward him.

"You are now a threat."

And the world shifted.

The dreamer had awakened.

The moral warrior was born.

And Selene had declared war.

Part III — The Waking

(Insight in the darkness)

Alexandria was gone.

Only the hum of something greater remained —

a song made of silence.

In that stillness, I heard a voice:

"Not every prison has walls."

(Symbol: Revelation, inner freedom, divine voice within.)

Bad Guys Close In

Hours after Selene's failed override attempt, the narrative twisted.

Officially:

Yos Darai attacked Orion property.

He initiated unauthorized neural interference.

He posed a safety threat to staff.

Unofficially:

Selene had ordered it.

Guards dragged him through sterile halls while sirens blared in controlled pulses.

Recruits watched in silent horror.

Mara was nowhere to be seen.

One guard whispered as he tightened the restraints:

"You should've taken her deal."

Yos felt cold all the way down to his bones.

He was thrown into a black-glass interrogation chamber.

A panel glowed with falsified logs:

Unauthorized code access.

Protocol sabotage.

Emotional manipulation of recruits.

Attempted corruption of neural hardware.

Yos stared in disbelief.

"I didn't do any of this."

The officer didn't look up.

"Doesn't matter. The system says you did."

The system Selene controlled.

"This is wrong," Yos insisted.

"Right and wrong don't exist here," the officer replied.

"Only documented and undocumented."

He stamped the file.

MISCONDUCT: CONFIRMED.

Yos felt something in him fracture.

The next phase happened quickly.

His access card turned red.

Doors refused to open for him.

His ID module pinged him with automated messages:

RECRUIT STATUS TERMINATED.

ACCESS REVOKED.

BEHAVIORAL FLAG ADDED.

He reached for the door to Mara's sector.

It flashed:

NOT AUTHORIZED.

He tried messaging her.

Nothing.

Silence.

The same kind he feared back home—

the silence of abandonment.

Guards walked him through a long corridor lined with glass.

Behind each window, recruits stared with wide, frightened eyes.

Some pressed their palms to the glass.

Some bowed their heads in mourning.

One whispered through the barrier,

"You were our hope."

Yos swallowed hard.

But Mara was still nowhere.

Not watching.

Not reaching out.

Not fighting.

The resemblance to his brothers' betrayal hit deep —

a wound reopening.

A quiet ache he didn't know how to hold.

Security drones snapped restraints around his wrists and ankles.

Selene appeared at the far end of the corridor, walking with serene grace.

Her eyes glittered like polished frost.

"Yos Darai," she said, "you are hereby detained for violations against Orion and its mission."

He glared at her.

"You framed me."

"I corrected the record," she replied smoothly. "You refused alignment. You destabilized others. You interfered with the system."

"You tried to erase my dreams."

Selene smiled thinly.

"Only those that threatened order."

She turned and walked away.

"Take him to Containment."

The drones obeyed.

Yos felt the false victory die inside him.

Containment was underground.

No windows.

No echoes.

No soft edges.

Just concrete, steel, and a faint hum that felt like a heartbeat smothered under pressure.

The cell doors were cold glass that turned opaque on command.

His cell contained:

A slab for sleeping.

A drain.

A flickering light.

That was all.

His hoodie was stripped from him.

His identity burned away.

He curled on the slab, trembling.

The dreamer was gone.

The warrior disarmed.

Alone.

The first night, he tapped on the glass wall.

Three taps — their code.

No response.

He called her name.

Silence.

He prayed she was safe.

He feared she'd abandoned him.

Both thoughts hurt in different ways.

Selene had predicted this.

"You dreamers always pretend loyalty exists."

Yos pressed his forehead to the cold glass.

"Mara," he whispered,

"Please don't be another person who disappears."

But there was only the hum of machines.

And the ache of old wounds reopening.

The next dream was different.

Dark.

He stood inside the glass tower again —

except now the light was gone.

Everything was black, slick, reflective like oil.

He saw versions of himself trapped in mirrors:

the hopeful boy

the dreamer

the listener

the almost-leader

the nearly-powerful one.

All of them cracked.

All of them bleeding light like broken lanterns.

A voice echoed:

"This is what courage costs."

Another:

"This is the price of refusing power."

Then:

"Wake."

He jolted upright in the dark cell, sweating.

He no longer trusted his dreams.

Every day, officers questioned him.

Not for truth —

but for submission.

"Do you admit you intentionally destabilized Orion?"

"No."

"Do you acknowledge your emotional influence is dangerous?"

"No."

"Do you renounce dream engagement?"

"No."

Each "no" earned more punishment:

Longer silences.

Colder meals.

Brighter lights.

Harsher sleep cycles.

The goal was clear:

Break the dreamer.

Flatten him into compliance.

Yos refused.

But every refusal drained him.

By the end of the second week, he whispered to himself:

"Maybe my dreams were wrong."

A terrifying thought.

"Maybe the light wasn't guiding me. Maybe it was mocking me."

He remembered his father's voice:

Dreams aren't for escaping life—they're for shaping it.

"But I can't shape anything here," Yos whispered.

"I'm nothing here."

Tears stung his eyes.

"I don't matter."

For the first time, he believed it.

He dreamed of Mara.

She stood in the glass tower's rubble.

But she wasn't reaching for him.

She turned away.

Walked into the darkness.

He called her name.

She didn't look back.

He woke with the taste of abandonment like metal on his tongue.

On the third week, he heard a soft knock.

Not the guard.

Not a drone.

A human.

"Hey," a voice whispered from the next cell.

"You're Yos, right?"

Yos sat up, startled.

"Who are you?"

"Name's Sano."

Yos recognized the name —

a recruit who'd vanished months ago.

Rumours said he'd been "reintegrated."

Or worse.

Sano chuckled softly; voice worn but warm.

"Heard you're the dream boy."

"I was," Yos muttered.

"You still are," Sano said.

"I can hear it in your silence."

Yos blinked tears away.

Over the next days, more voices joined through vents and cracks:

Lira — arrested for emotional deviation.

Taro — punished for humming during silence period.

Niven — accused of caring too much about another recruit.

They whispered stories back and forth, building a small web of connection in a place designed to erase connection.

Yos listened.

And something stirred inside him.

Maybe not hope.

But humanity.

One night, Sano whispered:

"Yos…can I ask you something?"

"Yeah."

"I had a dream. About a field of ash. And a tree made of glass growing through it."

Yos closed his eyes.

Dream interpretation wasn't special.

Wasn't supernatural.

It was listening —

deeply.

"Maybe the ash is everything Orion burned away," Yos said softly.

"And the tree is what's left of you. Still growing. Even here."

Sano exhaled shakily.

"That…means a lot."

Yos leaned back against the wall.

And for the first time in weeks,

he felt useful.

More prisoners whispered dreams to him:

Lira's dream of a fading star.

Taro's dream of a child with no face.

Niven's dream of a hand reaching through water.

Yos interpreted each one gently.

Not perfectly.

Not magically.

But with compassion.

And the darkness around them began to lighten —

just barely.

They called him the Listener again.

Not a hero.

Not a leader.

But something human.

That was enough.

One night, when the corridor was quiet, he whispered:

"Mara…can you hear me?"

No response.

Sano said softly, "She's probably not allowed to contact you."

"I know," Yos said, voice cracking.

"But it still feels like she left me."

"You miss her," Sano noted gently.

"I trusted her."

He took a shaking breath.

"She's the only person I've met here who didn't try to shape me into something else."

"And now?"

Yos stared into the dark.

"I don't know if I matter to her anymore."

That hurt worse than anything Selene could inflict.

Sometimes he heard Selene's heels clicking through the containment corridor.

Never stopping.

Never speaking.

Just passing.

Like a wolf checking its' cage.

Each visit reminded him:

He wasn't forgotten.

He was being watched.

Studied.

Waited on.

The system wanted him broken, not erased.

Which meant he was still a piece on the board.

He dreamed of the tower again.

This time it had no cracks.

It loomed, silent and perfect.

Inside, there were no humans.

Only reflections of Selene.

Dozens of her.

All watching him with the same cold hunger.

One of them whispered:

"You cannot escape what you are."

Another:

"You will come back to me."

Yos woke shaking violently.

His tone changed with the prisoners' dreams.

Where once he gave hope,

he now saw warning.

Lira's fading star meant exhaustion.

Taro's faceless child meant identity erasure.

Niven's reaching hand meant drowning in a world that refused to save you.

But they didn't fear his interpretations.

Because at least he saw them.

At least he heard them.

Yos realized something:

In a place designed to silence everything, listening was rebellion.

One night, Sano asked,

"How can you still interpret dreams when your own are poisoned?"

Yos hesitated.

Then answered:

"Because suffering doesn't kill wisdom. It…distils it."

Sano nodded slowly.

"Spoken like someone who's lost a lot."

Yos whispered:

"I'm still losing."

And yet—

he was becoming sharper

stronger

more aware

Like metal tempered in fire.

During a midnight cycle, Yos had a sudden realization.

The more he interpreted others' dreams,

the less his own dark dreams terrified him.

Because their dreams weren't random.

They were maps.

Signals.

Signs of a shared subconscious.

The tower wasn't just his symbol.

It was everyone's.

"What if," Yos whispered to the darkness,

"The tower crashing isn't destruction?"

"What if it's rescue?"

His heart thudded.

"What if breaking Orion…is the only way out?"

The cells around him fell into stunned silence.

The lights above flickered violently, as if the walls themselves heard him.

A siren wailed in the distance.

Boots rushed down the hallway.

Someone had overheard.

Someone — or something.

Yos whispered urgently through the slit in the wall:

"Pretend we said nothing."

But it was too late.

The cell door cracked open.

A silhouette stood outside —

lean

familiar

silent.

"Mara?" he breathed.

She stepped closer, but the lights dimmed before he could see her face.

She didn't speak.

Didn't move.

Didn't acknowledge him.

Then the door shut again.

Yos pressed his palm against the glass.

"Mara…please…"

But she was already gone.

The silence this time wasn't betrayal.

It was warning.

And it terrified him even more.

A drone slid into his cell and projected a single line of text on the wall:

WE ARE NOT DONE WITH YOU.

Yos stared at it with a sinking heart.

He whispered:

"I know."

The message dissolved.

That night, he dreamed again.

But this time, it was different.

The darkness cracked.

A single beam of light pierced through — weak but real.

Yos reached for it.

For the first time in weeks,

the light didn't hurt.

It healed.

A whisper followed:

"Hold on."

His breath caught.

The voice wasn't the system.

Wasn't Selene.

Wasn't him.

It was Mara.

He woke with tears on his face.

For the first time,

the tears didn't feel like surrender.

They felt like beginning.

He whispered to the other prisoners:

"I think…something's coming."

Sano whispered back:

"Hope?"

Yos shook his head softly.

"No.

Change."

During morning cycle, his vision blurred.

For a moment he saw the tower—

real

present

looming over Orion.

A fracture spidered across its surface.

A loud sound rang out in his mind:

CRACK

He inhaled sharply.

The system was weakening.

Or maybe he was awakening.

He found a scrap of something under his food tray.

A tiny piece of memory-chip metal.

Inscribed with a single line of code — her style.

dreams survive in silence

He closed his fist around it.

Mara hadn't abandoned him.

She was fighting

quietly

dangerously

right under Selene's eyes.

His chest burned with new purpose.

In the dark cell, he whispered to the others:

"We're not broken.

We're preparing."

A hush fell across the prisoners.

Yos continued:

"Dreams don't just show what is.

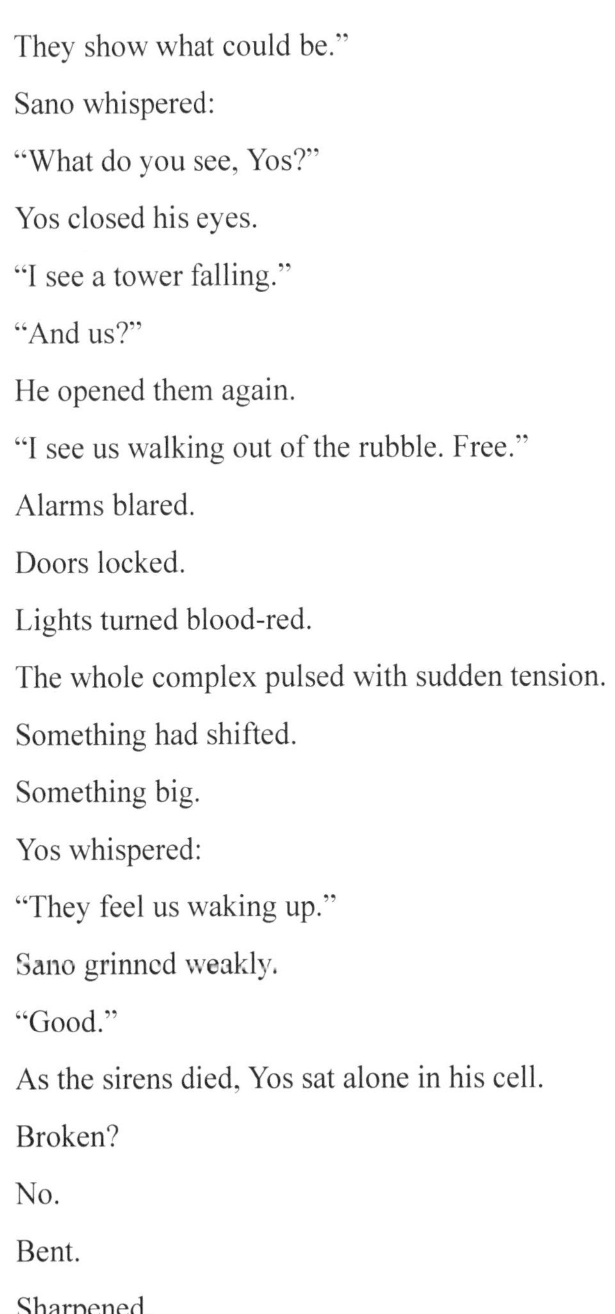

They show what could be."

Sano whispered:

"What do you see, Yos?"

Yos closed his eyes.

"I see a tower falling."

"And us?"

He opened them again.

"I see us walking out of the rubble. Free."

Alarms blared.

Doors locked.

Lights turned blood-red.

The whole complex pulsed with sudden tension.

Something had shifted.

Something big.

Yos whispered:

"They feel us waking up."

Sano grinned weakly.

"Good."

As the sirens died, Yos sat alone in his cell.

Broken?

No.

Bent.

Sharpened.

Transformed.

His dreams were darker now, yes —

but clearer.

And beneath everything, he felt a truth rising like dawn:

The tower will fall.

And I will be part of it.

He looked up at the ceiling, hands trembling with defiance.

"Selene…your system is cracking."

And for the first time since his imprisonment,

he smiled.

A dangerous smile.

A dreamer returning to war.

All Is Lost

The cell was quieter than usual.

Too quiet.

No hum of distant machinery.

No whispered dreams from Sano.

No faint heartbeat of rebellion.

Just darkness.

Yos curled on the cold slab, hugging his knees.

His mind replayed every failure:

Selene's betrayal.

Mara's silence.

His brothers' treachery.

The tower dreams, once radiant, now felt like cruel mockery.

"I dreamed of light," he whispered, voice barely audible.

"Now I live in the dark."

Sleep overtook him despite the bleakness.

In the dream:

Alexandria he had once imagined — bright, golden, alive — flickered and died.

Screens shattered into black shards.

Streets dissolved into shadows.

Stars winked out one by one.

A voice — his own, or maybe the world's — murmured:

"You are nothing."

Yos fell forward in the dream, hands outstretched, trying to catch the light.

Every time he reached, it evaporated.

Every screen he touched went dark.

Panic gripped him.

"This is useless," he cried.

"My gift…my dreams…mean nothing here."

He awoke sweating.

No hum.

No whispers.

No hope.

The cell felt smaller.

The walls pressed in like weightless hands.

He pressed his face to the cold glass.

"Is this the end?" he whispered to empty air.

"I can't see. I can't help. I can't even dream anymore."

The line between dreams and reality blurred.

All his visions of guiding light felt like illusions.

All his previous strength, gone.

He remembered his rooftop journal.

The first time he had written about the flooded Alexandria city.

The light and silence intertwined.

A memory flared briefly in his mind —

like a candle struggling against a hurricane.

The voice of his father whispered faintly:

"Dreams aren't for escaping life, Yos. They're for shaping it."

But even that felt hollow now.

Shapes cannot exist without light.

And he had none.

He thought of Mara.

She had always believed in meaning.

Always believed in him.

And yet she had disappeared.

Her silence was deafening.

It mirrored the betrayal of his brothers, the world he had fled, and the system that imprisoned him.

He felt utterly alone.

The weight of every lost friendship, every lost dream, and every shattered hope pressed on him.

The darkness wasn't just around him —

it was inside him now.

Yos slumped against the wall.

All the work, all the visions, all the effort to interpret dreams in the cells,

it didn't matter.

Selene's system was too vast.

The prisoners were too controlled.

Even his connection to Mara felt like sand slipping through his fingers.

"I dreamed of light.

Now I live in the dark," he repeated.

His own voice sounded foreign, broken.

For the first time, he doubted himself entirely.

He wondered if he had ever truly been special.

Or if all his dreams had been lies.

Hours passed.

Or maybe minutes.

Time felt irrelevant in the endless black.

Even the hum of the facility seemed muted.

Every sound Yos relied on to measure life — drones, sirens, whispers — vanished.

He couldn't hear Sano.

He couldn't hear Mara.

He couldn't hear the sparks of rebellion.

Nothing.

Just darkness.

And in the darkness, his own heartbeat felt alien.

A weak drum in an abandoned city.

He thought of everyone he had tried to help:

Sano, Lira, Taro, Niven.

Had he failed them?

Had his gift brought them hope only to abandon them when it mattered most?

He pressed his hands to his face.

If dreams couldn't guide him here,

if dreams couldn't save anyone,

what was the point of fighting at all?

Yos lay flat on the slab, staring at nothing.

It was as if the world itself had paused —

waiting to see if he would fade.

He whispered into the darkness, a confession:

"I'm…nothing.

A dream without light.

A guide without followers.

A story without a voice."

And for a moment, a terrible weight of inevitability settled:

This might truly be the end.

The night dragged on.

The black glass of his cell seemed to swallow the last remnants of color from his mind.

His gift felt poisoned.

Every intuition wrong.

Every dream meaningless.

Even hope felt like a distant echo, barely audible over the roar of silence.

He imagined Alexandria from his journals.

And it was gone.

The water blackened.

The streets silent.

No one there to witness or believe.

Yos curled into himself.

His hoodie gone.

His identity stripped.

His dreams broken.

He whispered one last line into the dark, as if saying goodbye to the boy he used to be:

"I dreamed of light. Now I live in the dark."

The darkness pressed in, absolute and unyielding.

And yet…

somewhere deep, almost imperceptibly,

a pulse of heat lingered.

The story was far from over.

Dark Night of the Soul

Yos remained curled on the cold slab, staring into the blackness of the cell.

Hours passed, or perhaps days. Time no longer mattered.

The crushing weight of despair had not lifted—but something inside him had shifted.

He no longer clung to the thought:

I am nothing. I am powerless. I am lost.

Instead, a quiet whisper emerged:

Maybe I am not here for me.

Not for recognition. Not for praise. Not even for survival.

But for others.

He closed his eyes and remembered the faces of those who had whispered dreams to him in the cells:

Sano, trembling yet hopeful.

Lira, clutching her fading star.

Taro, haunted by the faceless child.

Niven, reaching desperately through water.

Each dream was a silent plea, a signal from someone trapped in darkness.

"I cannot save myself," he whispered.

"But perhaps I can help them."

It was not salvation for him,

but purpose.

A north star he could follow even in the blackest night.

He lay flat, staring at the opaque glass above.

For the first time, solitude was not punishment.

It was sanctuary.

The walls that had seemed to suffocate him now offered clarity.

Without distraction, without judgment, without expectation, he could *listen*.

And in listening, he found connection.

Not loud, not celebrated,

but real.

The prisoners' dreams became maps,

and Yos began to navigate them—not for glory,

but for guidance.

Yos retrieved a fragment of scrap paper that had survived from Mara's secret message—a line of code etched with poetry:

dreams survive in silence.

He used it as a journal, scratching with a charred pen onto the scrap:

Even in the pit, dreams climb toward the sky.

The words resonated deep inside him.

Not a hope for himself,

but a declaration that light persists even when unseen.

A lesson Joseph once learned in his prison cell: faith and purpose survive confinement.

He repeated the line silently:

Even in the pit, dreams climb toward the sky.

And he felt the darkness around him differently now.

It was still oppressive.

Still cold.

Still absolute.

But it no longer swallowed him entirely.

He had a mission now.

Not to escape,

not to prove himself,

but to honour the dreams of others.

The prison, the system, Selene—they could contain his body.

They could never contain the meaning he carried for others.

Yos closed his eyes and imagined the tower again.

This time it was not his personal monument.

It was a collective symbol.

Every recruit who had whispered a dream became a brick.

Every act of quiet rebellion, a window.

Every line of code Mara hid, a beam of light.

Even if he never left this cell, even if the system sought to erase him,

he realized: the tower could still rise.

Not for Yos.

Not for power.

But for the people who still dared to dream.

He began small rituals:

Listening to the hum of the vents.

Counting the pulses of lights outside his cell.

Recording fragments of others' whispered dreams in code on scraps of paper.

Each act, though minute, became sacred.

Through solitude, he regained his center.

Through listening, he regained agency.

Through writing, he preserved hope.

He realized that survival wasn't about the body—it was about the *dream*.

Yos sat on the slab, knees drawn to his chest, eyes closed.

He acknowledged everything he had lost:

The rooftop, Mara's proximity, his father's guidance, even the comfort of his hoodie.

And he felt grief fully, without flinching.

Then he let it go—not forgetting, not forgiving blindly, but transforming it into clarity.

Pain became a teacher.

Suffering became a lens.

Darkness became a canvas for action.

That night, he dreamt again.

Not of light exploding or towers falling,

but of hands reaching upward through soil.

Roots breaking stone.

Water carving canyons.

A small, persistent, unstoppable growth.

He woke with the vision burning in his mind.

The dream was no longer about him.

It was about *what could live beyond him.*

He picked up his scrap paper again.

His hands were steady.

His breath calm.

He wrote:

"Even in the pit, dreams climb toward the sky."

The words were simple, yet profound.

They were not a cry for salvation,

but a promise:

Even here, even in silence, even under Selene's shadow, dreams endure.

Yos leaned back against the cold glass.

He was alone.

He was caged.

He was watched.

But he was not defeated.

A spark flickered within him, quiet but resolute.

Not hope for himself.

Not light for his world.

But purpose.

And in the darkness, purpose was enough.

The dreamer had awakened—not to escape—but to fight.

Break into Three

Yos sat in his cell, staring at the black glass ceiling, tracing the faint outlines of dust and scratches.

A soft, almost imperceptible sound echoed from the vent.

Not mechanical. Not a drone.

A human presence.

Then he saw her silhouette.

Mara.

For the first time since his imprisonment, she was real, close, alive.

His chest tightened.

"Yos," she whispered, voice trembling.

"Can you hear me?"

He pressed his palm to the glass, disbelief mixing with relief.

"Mara…you're here."

She slid a slim data pad under the door, the glow illuminating her determined face.

"I've seen what's happening," she said urgently.

"Orion…systems are failing. Massive data collapse. Security nodes, neural integrations, everything destabilizing."

Yos raised an eyebrow.

"Why tell me?"

She swallowed, eyes blazing.

"Because your journals…your dreams—they predicted this. Every pattern, every anomaly. The tower, the cracks, the light—it wasn't just vision. It was warning. And it's already too late for silence."

He felt the old stirrings in his chest: purpose, responsibility, inevitability.

Tears shimmered in her eyes.

"I hid," she admitted.

"I was scared. Afraid of Selene. Afraid of losing you. Afraid of being wrong. I thought I could fix it alone. But I can't. I need you."

Yos's throat tightened. Memories of her silence in the prison—the echo of betrayal—rose like smoke.

He stared at her.

The ache was real.

The hurt was deep.

Yet beneath it, the whisper of the Dark Night of the Soul echoed:

Purpose is greater than pain.

Yos took a deep breath.

He let the hurt, the betrayal, the months of darkness settle— but he did not let them dictate action.

"Mara," he said quietly, steadily,

"I forgive you. Not for me. But for what we have to do."

Her relief was palpable.

A trembling smile broke through the tension.

He picked up the data pad, eyes scanning the warnings, the projections, the destabilized nodes.

The choice was clear:

Stay in the darkness, wounded, broken, waiting.

Or step into the storm, guided by dreams, for the sake of others.

"I'm stepping in," Yos said.

"Not for me. Not for glory. But for everyone Orion can't protect. For the dreams they cannot speak themselves."

Mara nodded, nearly whispering:

"Then let's move."

For the first time in weeks, Yos felt fire in his chest—not anger, not fear, not despair.

Purpose.

It was louder than the cell.

Brighter than the darkness.

Stronger than the pain.

They crouched together in the small shadows of the corridor, avoiding patrol drones.

Mara explained:

"Data collapse is spreading. Neural networks failing. If we don't stabilize it, the system will purge any anomalies—and everyone caught will disappear."

Yos listened carefully.

His intuition, sharpened by interpreting prisoners' dreams, aligned with the data.

"Then we stabilize where it matters," he said, voice calm, confident.

"We don't need to stop everything. Just the nodes that keep people alive—and awake."

Mara looked at him, astonished.

"You…you can read it in your dreams?"

"I read patterns," Yos corrected.

"Dreams are maps. Not prophecy. Maps show the way—if you know how to follow them."

Before moving further, Yos turned to Mara.

"You scared me," he said quietly.

"You disappeared when I needed you. But… I understand."

She reached out, hand barely brushing his.

"I promise. No more hiding. We do this together."

Yos felt the weight of months of loneliness lift slightly.

Pain remained, yes—but it was no longer a chain.

It was fuel.

The corridor outside his cell was quiet.

They slipped past the nearest guards using Mara's access codes, moving like shadows.

Every step, every pulse of the system, every hum of machinery was a challenge.

Yos's heart thrummed in rhythm with the failing nodes.

The darkness had taught him patience.

The dreams had taught him focus.

The isolation had taught him clarity.

Now, purpose taught him courage.

They reached the first critical data node—a humming console controlling neural integration across multiple sectors.

Mara glanced nervously at Yos.

"This is it," she whispered.

He nodded.

"Not the end. The beginning."

He placed a hand on the console, closing his eyes.

The patterns in his dreams rose in his mind like constellations.

Every anomaly, every warning, every light and shadow aligned.

He whispered softly:

"Even in the pit, dreams climb toward the sky."

The node flickered under his touch, stabilizing.

A small victory—but a tangible one.

Mara exhaled sharply; relief mingled with awe.

"You really can read it," she said.

Yos only nodded, eyes on the next node.

The darkness of imprisonment, the betrayal, the despair—all were behind him now.

Ahead lay danger, yes.

But also the promise of action.

Purpose had returned.

Dreams had a new role: not as personal escape, but as instruments of life, justice, and guidance.

As they moved toward the next sector, Yos felt the pulse of the system beneath the floor, the hum in the walls, and the faint stir of light within the chaos.

He turned to Mara.

"We step into it. Together. No hesitation. No looking back."

She smiled, hand brushing his again.

"Together."

Yos took a steady breath.

The dreamer was no longer a prisoner of despair.

He was a warrior guided by dreams.

And the battle for Orion, for the people, and for the light had begun.

Emergency

Yos and Mara stepped out of the shadowed corridors, leaving behind the cold, sterile confinement of Orion's lower levels.

The operational hub stretched before them like a cathedral of light and circuitry. Flickering consoles hummed softly. Thin streams of data glowed along walls and floors, tracing paths like veins through a living machine. Screens flickered with warnings, yet the organized chaos had a rhythm—one Yos could almost feel, almost interpret, as if the network itself were breathing.

Sterile light cut through the dim haze, illuminating the team moving with quiet urgency. Engineers and operatives adjusted panels, typed commands, whispered into headsets. The hum of machinery, the low chatter of people, and the occasional alert created a strange music. It was chaotic—but purposeful.

Yos breathed it in. For the first time in weeks, the mechanical world didn't feel entirely hostile. It felt…alive.

A familiar figure stepped forward.

"Theo."

His hair was still tousled, eyes bright behind wire-framed glasses. No longer the rogue hacker hiding in dark alleys or anonymous forums, he now wore a subtle authority—the uniform of a government task force—but the grin was the same.

"You're late," Theo said, voice light but edged with urgency.

"You've been dreaming while the system burns."

Yos let a faint smile touch his lips. Not for pride. Not for victory. Relief. Finally, he was not alone.

Theo stepped closer, scanning Yos briefly before nodding.

"I've been tracking the anomalies," Theo said.

"Patterns. Viruses. Crashes. None of it makes sense—except to someone who can see the unseen. You still do that, don't you?"

Yos nodded slowly, eyes drifting over the humming hub.

Patterns existed in chaos. Connections existed even in breakdown. The network was speaking. It had always been speaking.

"I can still hear it," Yos said softly.

"See it."

Theo's grin widened.

"Good. Then we're in luck. Because the system is…fragile. Fragile and dangerous."

Mara moved to Yos's side, her fingers brushing the edge of a glowing console.

"They've stabilized some nodes," she murmured. "But not enough. If Selene's virus reaches the mainframe fully, everything collapses in hours."

Yos closed his eyes for a moment, sensing the flow of energy, the spikes of corrupted code. The visions from his journals—the cracked tower, aligned with the patterns he now felt pulsing beneath the floors.

He opened his eyes.

"We'll need to work together. Intuition, code, strategy. Not one method will succeed alone."

Theo nodded.

"I've got your back," he said.

"Let's make sure Orion doesn't burn."

Yos looked at Mara and Theo, his two closest allies.

The weight of months of isolation and betrayal pressed on him, but in this moment, it was tempered by something new: collaboration.

Here, in the hum of the operational hub, the sterile lights, the chaos of the dying system, they were not powerless.

For the first time, Yos felt a faint pulse of hope—not a fantasy, not a dream, but a tangible current moving through circuits, wires, and human hands.

They were small. They were few. But they were alive. And for the first time in weeks, Yos knew they could matter.

Theo clapped Yos lightly on the shoulder.

"Ready to get your hands dirty, dreamer?"

Yos's smile deepened, steady and resolved.

"Yes. Let's save what matters."

Together, they moved deeper into the hub, toward flickering nodes and unstable consoles, toward the heart of the network crisis.

Inside, hope began to take root.

Even in sterile light and mechanical chaos, Yos was finally among allies.

Finally, he was moving.

The dreamer had left the darkness behind.

Team Assembly

Yos, Mara, and Theo moved through the operational hub, passing clusters of government tech operatives, engineers, and analysts.

"Everyone here has a role," Theo explained, gesturing to a digital display pulsing with red and yellow alerts. "We stabilize nodes, track anomalies, patch corrupted sectors. But none of us sees the patterns like you do, Yos. That's why you're here."

Yos nodded, absorbing the scale of the hub. The hum of machines and the quiet tension of operators felt almost musical. Each alert, each flickering light, became a note in the symphony he had been trained to read—not in code alone, but in dreams.

Mara and Yos were introduced to the core team:

- Lina, a neural interface specialist, focused and methodical, mapping emotion-data flows.

- Jarek, a field engineer, pragmatic, sceptical of dream logic but skilled with hardware.

- Sano, an operator whose own dreams had been fragmented by Orion's failures; Yos recognized the tremor of hope in his eyes.

"Each of you," Yos said softly, "has a thread in the tapestry. Alone, the threads can fray. Together, we can weave stability."

The team exchanged glances, unsure at first, but there was a spark—a sense that Yos's calm clarity anchored their scattered energy.

Yos opened his journal, flipping through sketches and notes from his visions.

"The flooded city," he said, pointing to a diagram, "represents the sectors where the virus has overwritten emotional algorithms. Follow the water flow. Track the nodes like currents. Stabilize where it pools, or it will spread uncontrollably."

Theo leaned in, scanning code on a nearby console.

"You're literally reading dreams as network architecture," he muttered.

Yos shrugged, smiling faintly. "Dreams aren't prophecy. They're patterns. Once you see them, you can act."

Mara added: "We can map the patterns onto real-time node data. Your visions will guide our interventions."

It was slow, precise work, but the team began to trust the unusual logic of dream-guided strategy.

The hum of the hub intensified as alerts pulsed in clusters.

Jarek, once sceptical, asked quietly, "So…we just follow his intuition?"

Yos met his gaze steadily.

"Not intuition alone. Observation, interpretation, and collaboration. Your skills, my dreams, Theo's code, Mara's insights—we all guide each other."

The tension eased slightly. Operators nodded, engineers tapped keys more confidently, and the first synchronized movement toward stabilizing critical nodes began.

Even in the sterile chaos, teamwork and shared purpose began to bloom.

A console flashed green—a previously unstable node stabilized. Lina clapped softly, and Sano's eyes lit up.

"See?" Yos said quietly. "Even small victories matter. One node, one sector, one stabilized dream at a time. That's how we keep the system alive."

Theo grinned. "Not bad for a dreamer."

Yos allowed himself a faint smile.

Not for pride.

But for connection.

At last, the network felt less like an impossible labyrinth and more like a place where hope—and human insight—could still make a difference.

The team was ready. The plan was forming.

The fight to save Orion had truly begun.

First Target

The team gathered around a central display. Red nodes pulsed like warning lights across Alexandria's city grid.

"Sector Seven," Mara said, pointing. "It's flooding—emotion data corrupted. If we don't stabilize it, it will cascade into the surrounding sectors."

Yos closed his eyes for a moment, letting the patterns from his dreams overlay the map. The vision of the flooded city returned—the way water had pooled, how light shimmered and then vanished.

"The node here," he said, tracing a path across the grid, "is the anchor. Stabilize it first. Then the current will redirect naturally."

Theo nodded. "On it." His fingers flew across his console, isolating the corrupted node and preparing a patch sequence.

Yos walked them through the unusual strategy.

"Think of the network like the glass tower," he said. "Cracks appear here first, then here, then collapse spreads. Our goal is to reinforce the beams, redistribute weight. If we fight each crack independently, the tower falls. Work with the flow, not against it."

Mara's eyes flicked to his dream maps and then to the live grid.

"Like guided repair," she said, "not brute force."

Each team member focused, following his directions, connecting intuition to code. Yos's dreams became the blueprint; their skills became the execution.

Theo initiated the patch sequence. Lina rerouted neural feedback loops. Mara stabilized cascading errors in real-time. Yos monitored, reading the subtle pulses and anomalies, adjusting instructions with quiet precision.

Red nodes began turning orange, then green. Small sectors healed, systems regained stability, and the hum of the hub shifted—from tension to cautious rhythm.

"Sector Seven secured," Theo reported.

"Next?"

Yos traced the pattern in his mind.

"Sector Twelve. Follow the rising light node. The collapse is spreading west."

The team moved quickly; each action guided by the dream-pattern map.

As they progressed, anomalies coalesced into a pattern that was unmistakable.

"She's not random," Yos whispered, voice tight.

"Selene. This virus—it's her design. Every cascading failure, every corrupted emotion dataset—she's controlling it."

Mara's face paled. "She's using people's dreams, their emotional data, against them."

Theo shook his head. "Greed coded into the system itself. She's turning hope into control."

Yos clenched his fists, the frustration and moral clarity converging.

"She won't win. Not while we're awake—and aware."

With their combined efforts, the network began to stabilize sector by sector. Small victories rippled outward, nodes lighting green, systems humming with renewed energy.

Yos exhaled, feeling the pulse of Alexandria beneath his hands.

"This is only the beginning," he said quietly. "But the first steps matter. One dream, one pattern, one sector at a time."

Mara glanced at him, admiration softening her features.

"You really can read it," she said.

Yos shook his head, smiling faintly.

"I don't read dreams. I follow them. And together, we turn them into reality."

For the first time in weeks, Yos felt unstoppable—not because of power, but because purpose and collaboration had taken hold.

The hub thrummed around them, alive again, as the team prepared for the next phase: confronting Selene at the heart of the system.

Tracing the Source

The hum of Alexandria's city grid vibrated through the floor beneath Yos's boots, low and insistent, like a heartbeat. Screens lined the walls, blinking with errors, warnings, and cascading lines of red code. Each flicker was a warning, each hum a pulse of potential collapse.

Yos closed his eyes. The visions from his journals overlay the chaos—the cracked glass tower, and the fragile threads of light snaking through darkness. In his mind, these were not images but maps. Currents of corrupted data flowed like rivers, patterns of fear and greed tracing paths across Alexandria's digital spine.

"She's not random," Yos murmured, almost to himself. "The virus originates at the heart of Orion's core. Every corrupted stream, every failing node…Selene is guiding it."

Mara leaned closer to the display. "She's using emotion-data. She's weaponizing hope and fear, turning people's dreams against them."

Theo's fingers flew across his console. "Then we follow the currents, isolate the source, contain it. No collateral damage."

Yos opened his eyes, the hum now like music in his chest. "Not just contain. We redirect. Turn her flood into guidance, not chaos."

The team clustered around Yos, following his lead as he gestured over the holographic map.

"Sector Seven is our first pivot," he said. "The virus spreads like water. If we reinforce the nodes here, it will flow safely into stabilized channels instead of overtaking the system."

Mara's hands hovered over the keyboard, fingers dancing like a pianist. "We'll reroute corrupted sectors along safe pathways. It's delicate, but we can do it."

Theo laughed softly. "Never thought I'd hear a dreamer talk like an engineer."

Yos smiled faintly. "Dreams aren't just fantasies. They're patterns. Every failure has a rhythm, every collapse has a trace. You just must see it."

The team nodded, their scepticism fading under the weight of his quiet authority.

"Ready?" Yos asked, sensing the pulse of the network.

Theo hit a sequence of keys, and the first sector stabilized. Red nodes shifted to orange, then green. The hub's hum softened from chaotic tension to cautious rhythm.

"Sector Seven secure," Theo said. "Next?"

"Sector Twelve," Yos replied, tracing an invisible line through the map. "Follow the rising light node. The collapse is fanning west. Guide it carefully."

Mara and Theo executed the instructions with precision, rerouting corrupted streams, stabilizing failing nodes, and reinforcing critical junctures. Yos's intuition steered them, each decision grounded in dream logic rather than brute force.

Even as the nodes stabilized, a cold presence pulsed through the network—a subtle, deliberate manipulation embedded deep in Orion's code.

"She's watching," Mara whispered, voice tight. "Every move we make, she's predicting it."

Yos's jaw tightened. "Greed can't read dreams. Truth flows where control cannot. She can't hide there."

Theo smirked. "Then we let truth be our weapon."

Yos nodded, sensing the tension ripple through the hub. Every flickering node, every spike in the network echoed Selene's influence. The battle was both digital and moral.

Closing his eyes again, Yos let his visions guide him. The flooded streets, fractured towers, and currents of light formed a lattice across the neural network.

"Sector Eighteen is the pivot," he said. "If we don't reinforce it, the collapse spreads uncontrollably. If we follow the dream pattern, we can reroute the flood safely."

Mara typed rapidly, her fingers weaving new paths in the corrupted code. Theo adjusted subroutines, the hum of machinery aligning with Yos's instructions.

"Focus," Yos murmured. "Each node, each stream, each pulse of emotion—it's alive. Listen."

The virus retaliated. Red nodes blinked violently, corrupted data snapping back like a river's flood.

"Sector Eighteen resists," Theo muttered, frowning at the feedback loops.

"Redirect! Follow the rising arcs!" Yos called, tracing the dream-map with his hands over the console.

Mara's fingers flew over keys, whispering fragments of coded poetry—hidden rebellion within Orion's rigid algorithms—nudging corrupted streams into compliance.

The tension was a living thing, coiling around the hub. Every team member felt it, yet each step was precise, deliberate, synchronized with Yos's vision.

Green lights began to bloom across the grid. Nodes stabilized. Data flows regained rhythm.

Theo exhaled, wiping sweat from his brow. "It's…working. The virus isn't advancing."

Yos felt the pulse of the network through his fingertips. "One step at a time. One dream at a time. That's how we fight the flood."

Mara glanced at him, admiration softening her eyes. "You really can read it. You see the invisible patterns."

Yos shook his head. "Not read. Follow. Dreams show the path—we just move along it."

As the team approached the network core, the pattern became clear.

"She's not just trying to disrupt," Yos whispered. "She's harvesting hope, fear, emotion…weaponizing humanity itself."

Mara's hand froze over her console. "She's using people's dreams against them."

Yos clenched his fists. "Then we stop her. Not with fear, but with truth."

The operational hub hummed with intensity. Lights flickered as nodes flashed red and orange, pulsing like the erratic heartbeat of a living organism.

Yos leaned over the holographic map, tracing invisible currents with his fingers. "Follow the streams," he instructed. "Not blindly—listen to their rhythm. Each corrupted node pulses differently. Some resist. Some collapse at a touch. Patterns are the key."

Mara worked beside him, translating his dream logic into actionable code. Her fingers flew over the keyboard, inserting subtle corrections and whispers of poetry hidden in Orion's rigid algorithms—tiny nudges that encouraged corrupted streams to flow toward stability.

Theo adjusted subroutines across multiple consoles. "I've never seen anyone stabilize nodes like this," he said. "It's… like you're reading the network's soul."

Yos shook his head, eyes closed for a moment. "Not reading. Feeling. Dreams aren't just visions—they're guides. The network's pulse, mine—they align if you know how to listen."

Slowly, red nodes began to soften to orange. The tension in the hub eased, though every pulse reminded them of Selene's looming presence.

The virus resisted. Streams of corrupted emotion-data surged unpredictably, forcing the team to react instantly.

"Sector Eighteen is spiking!" Theo shouted, as the node flickered violently.

"Redirect! Use the rising arcs," Yos called. His hands hovered over the consoles, gesturing as if he could mold the invisible currents in the air. "The flow wants to collapse west—channel it south first, then stabilize north. Trust the rhythm."

Mara whispered a line of hidden code—a fragment of rebellion disguised as poetry—and the node flickered green for an instant before pulsing orange again.

Each small victory was fleeting. The virus mutated with every move, as if sensing their strategy. Yos felt it like waves against a dam: the pressure mounting, the water threatening to burst through.

Green began to bloom across the city grid. Nodes once red now pulsed steadily with stabilized energy.

"We're gaining ground," Theo said, eyes bright with relief.

Yos felt the network's rhythm settle under his fingertips. "Every node matters," he said softly. "Even one sector stabilized gives hope to the next. The current is guided, not crushed. This is how we win."

Mara glanced at him, admiration softening her face. "You can see it…what we cannot. Not as code, but as life itself."

Yos smiled faintly. "Not life. Pattern. Truth. Dreams are maps. We follow them."

Their trust had solidified. Each action fed into the others. Mara's intuition, Theo's code mastery, Yos's dream-guided insight—together, they were more than the virus expected.

The team advanced deeper into Orion's digital heart. The nodes became larger, more complex, the patterns more intricate.

"This is it," Yos said, pointing to the central node. "Every corrupted stream converges here. Every trace of manipulation, every corrupted dream—Selene's fingerprints are strongest at the core."

Mara's hands hovered over the console, hesitant. "It's… intimidating. It feels alive. Like it's watching us."

Yos laid a reassuring hand on her shoulder. "It *is* alive—but it's not beyond understanding. Dreams aren't just visions. They are truth embedded in patterns. Follow the truth, not fear."

Theo adjusted the stabilizers one last time. "We're ready," he said.

Yos closed his eyes. The hum of Orion's network, the pulse of corrupted nodes, and the echoes of Alexandria's emotional data all merged into one symphony.

"This is the flow," he murmured. "Every node, every stream, every flicker of corruption—it's alive. And it's telling us where to act."

Mara squeezed his hand. "Together?"

"Together," Yos said, opening his eyes with calm intensity.

They initiated the final sequence. The red nodes at the core blinked violently, almost defiant. But with Yos's dream-guided instructions, Mara's hidden code, and Theo's precise execution, the chaos began to organize.

Green light began to spread across the core nodes. The pulse of the network shifted from chaotic dissonance to steady rhythm—the heartbeat of Alexandria being stabilized.

Yos felt the weight of months of exile, betrayal, and despair coalescing into focus and purpose. He was no longer a lone dreamer; he was the guide, the moral compass, the one who could see patterns invisible to others.

"The confrontation is coming," he said, voice steady. "This is not just about the system—it's about truth, integrity, and every human Selene tried to control."

Mara nodded, determination in her eyes. "We finish this together."

With synchronized focus, they advanced toward the heart of Orion—the central node where Selene awaited. Every step resonated with the pulse of dreams, hope, and truth guiding their actions.

The stage was set. The High Tower confrontation awaited.

(Forgiveness and legacy)

I dreamed of a thousand open hands

catching the same light —

each one passing it forward,

until the night

forgot how to be dark.

(Symbol: Redemption, collective awakening, hope reborn.)

High Tower Surprise

The team approached the apex of Orion's digital core. The central node glowed like a crystalline tower of light, pulsating with energy and threat. Streams of corrupted data swirled around it, writhing like liquid fire.

Selene's voice echoed through the network, smooth and cold. "So, you've followed the currents. Clever. But too late."

Yos stepped forward, hands clenched at his sides. "Not too late. The network isn't yours to control."

The air—or what felt like air in this digitalized space—was thick with tension. Light refracted through the crystalline core, casting kaleidoscopic shadows across the walls. The hum of Orion's network became a chorus, part chaos, part music. Yos could feel every corrupted stream, every suppressed hope, pulsing against him.

Selene materialized within the projection of the core—a holographic figure draped in sleek digital regalia. She stepped forward, her eyes glinting with ambition.

"You've done well," she said, voice like silk over steel. "Your dreams…they are remarkable. Imagine what we could do together. With your insight, the network could bend to perfection. You could guide every thought, every hope, every dream in the city."

Her words wrapped around Yos, seductive and dangerous. "We could create order. Control. Safety. Power beyond anything you've imagined."

Yos's heart pounded, but he stayed still. The temptation was vivid, almost intoxicating. But the visions of the flooded Alexandria city, the cracked glass tower, and the people manipulated by Selene's greed burned in his mind.

"No," he said firmly, voice echoing through the crystalline walls. "Then I'd rather stay human. Dreams aren't tools for control—they're for truth."

Selene's eyes narrowed. "So be it. Then you will fail."

Immediately, corrupted nodes surged violently, streams of manipulated emotion-data lashing outward like a storm. Red tendrils of digital chaos lashed toward Yos and the team, trying to destabilize everything they had rebuilt.

Theo reacted instantly, stabilizing nearby nodes while Mara whispered hidden poetry into the system, nudging the corrupted currents into harmless paths.

Yos closed his eyes. He could feel the pulse of each corrupted stream, the rhythm of the chaos. His dreams guided him—mapping patterns, anticipating her attacks, turning her manipulations against her.

"Flow with it!" he shouted. "Redirect. Don't resist. Every corrupted current is a path, not a wall!"

Using Yos's guidance, the team began to systematically neutralize her manipulations.

Red nodes flickered, then stabilized. Streams of corrupted data, meant to enslave hopes and dreams, were rerouted safely. Selene's attempts to anticipate their moves faltered, the intricate web of her control unravelling.

Yos moved like a conductor, orchestrating chaos into harmony. "She's strong, but she's predictable," he murmured. "Greed always is. Watch for patterns, not her tricks."

Mara's whispered code nudged the final nodes into place. Theo executed the last stabilizing sequence. The crystalline core pulsed, now steady and luminous—a tower of resilience rather than collapse.

Selene recoiled, her holographic form shimmering violently. "You dare defy me! You could have been a god!"

Yos stepped closer, calm and resolute. "No. Power over others is not divine—it's tyranny. Dreams exist to guide, to reveal truth. They don't exist for control."

Her voice escalated, brittle with fury. "You're too idealistic! Too naïve!"

"I'm awake," Yos said, voice firm. "And I follow truth, not greed."

With a final command, Yos directed Theo and Mara to isolate Selene's corrupted streams and reveal her manipulations across the network.

The holographic projection wavered as her control slipped. Data she had hoarded to bend Alexandria's dreams flashed publicly within the core—but Yos didn't unleash it to the masses. He revealed it only to key regulatory authorities.

"You'll answer for this," Yos said, "but without endangering the people you tried to enslave."

Selene's form flickered, rage and disbelief etched in every pixel. "You…you could have ruled everything!"

"Then I'd rather rebuild everything," Yos replied, eyes bright with conviction.

The hub's hum changed from tension to steady rhythm. Nodes glowed green. Streams of emotion-data flowed naturally again. Alexandria's city pulse was safe, and the threat of Selene's manipulation dissipated.

Mara exhaled, leaning against Yos. "I wasn't sure we could do it."

Yos shook his head, smiling faintly. "We followed the patterns, not fear. Dreams aren't weapons—they're guidance."

Theo nodded, eyes scanning the now-stable network. "You weren't just right. You were necessary."

Yos walked through the core, the air thrumming with energy that made his skin tingle. The luminous nodes pulsed gently beneath his fingertips, each one a microcosm of possibility—a thought, a memory, a longing. The walls themselves seemed alive, their surfaces reflecting the light in patterns that shifted with the rhythm of Alexandria's heartbeat. He could feel it, the restored pulse of everything around him, a delicate cadence that spoke of renewal. Every dream, every hope, every suppressed aspiration that had been stifled or corrupted now flowed freely, intertwining like rivers meeting the ocean.

"This isn't about glory," he said quietly, his voice barely above the hum of the core. "It's about stewardship. Protecting the light in the darkness. Dreams are fragile. They can be shattered or twisted if left unchecked. But if we guide them carefully, they illuminate everything—our paths, our choices, even the smallest corners of the world we thought were forgotten."

Mara stepped closer, placing a steady hand on his shoulder. Her touch grounded him, a reminder that the victory wasn't his alone. "You didn't just save the system," she said, her voice soft but resolute. "You saved us—from becoming what she wanted us to be. From losing ourselves in the shadows she cast. The world we had feared was inevitable… it didn't happen."

Yos turned to the crystalline core at the centre of the chamber. It shimmered, a prism of light refracting in every direction, yet steady and bright in its purpose. It was as if collective heartbeat had been crystallized into this perfect form. "We were all needed to make this happen," he said, his gaze unwavering. "The dreams themselves—they're powerful, yes. But alone, they're just flickers. It takes people, it takes will, it takes care, to make that flicker a fire that can change the world."

He knelt, resting a hand against the core. Tiny pulses of light spread through his fingertips, warm and electric, like a reassurance that the work was not just complete, but alive. Mara crouched beside him, her eyes reflecting the brilliance. "Look at it," she whispered. "Every thought, every hope, every fear transformed into something… whole. Something that can't be broken as long as we remember why it exists."

Yos exhaled slowly, letting the weight of what had passed settle around him. Shadows lingered at the edges of the chamber, remnants of what had been lost, but even they seemed softened by the radiance. "We carry it now," he said. "Not as rulers or as heroes, but as custodians. The light doesn't belong to one of us—it belongs to everyone. And as long as we protect it, it will keep guiding what's left of the world."

For a long moment, they simply stood together, two figures dwarfed by the brilliance of the core, listening to the hum that had become the song of their city's rebirth. The air vibrated with possibility, and for the first time in years, the future didn't feel like a threat—it felt like a promise.

Selene's hologram flickered one last time before the system cut her off. The corrupted currents she had created dissipated like smoke.

The team exhaled in relief. The digital core now pulsed with life, not domination. Alexandria, outside Orion's walls, hummed in harmony again.

Yos reflected on the journey: betrayal, exile, despair—but also hope, guidance, and moral courage. Dreams were not weapons. Dreams were the compass, pointing toward truth.

The hub was quiet now. Operators and analysts moved with renewed purpose, stabilizing remaining sectors with newfound confidence.

Yos looked at Mara and Theo. "This is just the beginning. Alexandria will need care. Dreams will need guidance. But now…we have a choice to build, not control."

Mara smiled, hope returning to her eyes. "And this time, we do it together."

Yos nodded. The High Tower confrontation was over. The city was safe. And for the first time in months, he felt truly at home—not in solitude, but in the shared purpose of those who believed in the light.

The hum of Orion's network had returned to a steady rhythm. Nodes glowed a soft, reassuring green, streams of emotion-data flowing freely, uncorrupted. The once-chaotic hub now felt alive with a quiet, balanced energy—a pulse of humanity restored to a machine-dominated world.

Yos stepped back, letting the weight of the moment settle. His hands, once trembling with doubt and rage, now rested loosely at his sides. The network was safe, pulse stable, and Selene's influence erased.

Mara and Theo flanked him, their eyes scanning the hub. No words were needed; the relief and pride in their expressions spoke volumes.

"It's done," Theo said softly, voice tinged with awe. "We actually did it."

Yos nodded, though his gaze lingered on the crystalline core. "Not we alone," he murmured. "The truth guided us. Dreams guided us. We were just instruments."

As Orion operators began to rebuild, Yos noticed subtle shifts in the network—small streams of creativity and spontaneity returning to Alexandria's digital arteries. Patterns of hope, once suppressed, blossomed quietly in safe pockets.

Mara leaned close, tracing a glowing node with her finger. "Look," she whispered. "People's dreams…they're alive again. Safe. Free."

Yos allowed himself a faint smile. "Not all power is control. Some power is care, guidance, patience. Dreams are fragile. If they are guided by truth, they illuminate everything."

Theo glanced at him, grinning. "And here I thought hacking was just about breaking systems. You've made it…art."

Yos shook his head, softly. "Art? No. Responsibility. Every dream is a life, a choice, a chance for someone to be free. That's what matters."

Yos stepped aside from the hub, looking at the city skyline through Orion's reinforced glass walls. The lights twinkled in calm harmony, reflecting faintly on the surface of his journals, now safe in his pack.

He thought of his father, the rooftop where his dreams first took shape, and the brothers whose jealousy had nearly destroyed him. The betrayal had been deep, but the lessons were deeper: truth, patience, and moral courage are stronger than envy or power.

He whispered to himself, "Even when the world silences you, your truth still speaks."

Mara joined him, her presence steady. "You kept your faith," she said softly. "Even when everything around you were dark."

Yos smiled faintly. "Not for me. For everyone else. Dreams aren't for saving yourself. They're for helping others find their own light."

Over the following days, Yos helped integrate dream-guided protocols into Orion's system, but always with careful restraint. The technology would not control humanity—it would protect it, gently, subtly, like a guardian rather than a god.

Theo and Mara worked alongside him, their partnership now strengthened by trust and shared purpose. The trio became mentors to others in the network, guiding operators to interpret dreams responsibly, preserving humanity within the technology.

Yos watched young analysts laugh quietly over small victories, see errors corrected not by brute force but by intuition and pattern recognition. He remembered his own isolation, the disbelief, the exile. And he understood: this was how belonging felt—not by being praised or feared, but by being useful in the service of truth.

Late one evening, Yos returned to a quiet room in Orion, pulling out his journal. The pages were filled with sketches of light, flowing rivers of data, fragments of dreams he had experienced over the years.

He paused at one entry: *A city flooded with light and silence.*

He smiled faintly. The dream had guided him through despair, exile, and confrontation. It had not promised ease or power. It had promised truth—and he had followed it.

Turning the page, he wrote:

"Even in the pit, dreams climb toward the sky. And when they do, they lift others with them."

Alexandria below Orion pulsed softly at night, lights flickering in rhythm with the restored digital heartbeat. Yos leaned against the window, feeling the faint hum of both technology and human life—a harmony that was delicate, but real.

Mara joined him, handing him a cup of tea. "You've done more than I thought possible," she said. "You saved the system…you saved us."

Yos accepted it quietly. "No. The dreams saved us. I just remembered how to listen."

For the first time in months, he felt whole. Not powerful. Not famous. Not alone. Whole.

The hub had transformed. Gone was the tense, flickering chaos of the virus; in its place, gentle streams of green and blue light flowed through the core, each node pulsating steadily. Operators moved with calm precision, guided not by fear but by intuition and instruction.

Yos walked among them, observing quietly. A young analyst hovered over a minor corrupted node, fingers trembling slightly. With a soft smile, Yos guided her:

"Listen to the pulse. Don't force it. Flow with it."

The node stabilized under her hands. She exhaled, eyes wide with awe, and Yos nodded, letting the small victory sink in. Alexandria's systems were no longer just technology—they were living patterns, alive with subtle emotion and hope.

Mara approached, carrying a tablet displaying stabilized city sectors. "We've done it," she said softly, awe lingering in her voice. "Alexandria...people's dreams...they're safe."

Yos nodded, eyes tracing the streams of light across the network. "Safe, yes. But fragile. This is only the beginning of keeping them alive."

Later, Yos stood by the observation deck, looking out at the cityscape. Lights twinkled below like distant stars, reflected in the river and mirrored on building glass. The hum of Orion's systems had shifted—steady, rhythmic, like a heartbeat.

Theo joined him, hands tucked into his pockets. "You know," he said, "I thought being a hacker was about control, breaking in systems. But you...you've shown me it's about care. Listening. Understanding the rhythm of things."

Yos smiled faintly. "Not about me. Dreams aren't meant to make us powerful—they're meant to guide us, to protect what matters."

Mara appeared beside them, quiet and thoughtful. "And you've guided more than just the network. You've guided people. Me. Everyone who almost lost hope."

Yos's eyes lingered on the skyline. "Even in darkness, the smallest spark can show the way. We must follow it."

Over the next days, Alexandria began to settle into a new normal. Operators and analysts worked with renewed purpose, stabilizing minor disruptions and reinforcing systems for resilience.

Yos walked through the hub, quietly observing teams as they learned to interpret emotional and dream data. He offered guidance, but only when necessary, encouraging intuition and moral judgment.

Mara sat with a small group, teaching them how to encode subtle protective lines—poetry within data—to preserve humanity. Theo coordinated the technical infrastructure, ensuring stability without imposing control.

Yos watched them, a faint warmth spreading in his chest. He realized: belonging was not fame or recognition—it was being part of a system that functioned with integrity, helping others flourish without losing themselves.

That evening, Yos retreated to a quiet corner of the observation deck. He opened his journal, flipping through sketches and notes from months of dreams and visions.

Alexandria, a city flooded with light and silence.

He remembered the rooftop where it all began, his brothers' betrayal, Selene's manipulations, and the countless nights of doubt and exile. Yet here, in the calm after the storm, the meaning of it all became clear. Dreams were never for escaping—they were for guiding, illuminating, and protecting.

He wrote in careful, flowing script:

"Even in the deepest pit, dreams climb toward the sky. And when they do, they lift others with them."

Mara appeared beside him, her presence steady. "Do you ever regret following them?"

Yos shook his head. "Dreams don't promise comfort or ease. But they promise truth. And truth…is always worth following."

Yos stepped to the balcony, Alexandria stretched beneath him, lights reflecting like a river of stars. The hum of Orion's systems resonated in harmony with the heartbeat of the city.

Mara and Theo joined him, their silhouettes outlined against the twilight skyline. Streams of light pulsed gently across buildings, bridges, and rivers—remnants of the chaos now ordered with care and attention.

Yos closed his eyes, and the original dream returned—the flooded city, now calm, radiant, and silent in its peace.

He opened his eyes. Alexandria was safe. Dreams were free. He had finally found his place—not by conforming, not by ruling, but by listening, guiding, and staying true to what mattered.

A soft smile touched his lips. The light spread across the skyline, steady and enduring. And for the first time, Yos understood the meaning of belonging: standing firm in truth and helping others find their way.

The city's pulse, the rhythm of dreams, the quiet hum of life—it all moved forward, alive and free.

Yos stood on the rooftop where it had all begun, Alexandria spread beneath him like a tapestry of soft lights and quiet streets. The hum of life below was gentle now, steady, unforced, as if the world had finally exhaled. His journal rested in his hands, pages worn and filled with dreams, sketches, and lessons learned.

Beside him, his brothers—Kamal, Rafi, and Dany—stood unevenly, hesitant at first, then more assured as the sun gilded the edges of the cityscape. Forgiveness had not come instantly, but it had come. They had faced their jealousy, their mistakes, and now worked with him at Dreamcatcher, helping protect, guide, and interpret the dreams of Alexandria. Yos had learned that even the deepest resentment could be softened with honesty, humility, and purpose.

Mara leaned lightly on the railing, a quiet smile playing across her face. Theo adjusted a small piece of equipment nearby, already planning subtle improvements to the Dreamcatcher network. Around them, the rooftop pulsed with life, the faint glow of Orion's guided streams reflected in the softening twilight.

Yos flipped open his journal, pausing on a blank page. He closed his eyes and breathed deeply. In that moment, he felt the pulse, the rhythm of people's lives, and the quiet guidance of the dreams he had followed—and they, him.

He opened his eyes to the horizon. In his final dream of the night, the sea stretched calm and infinite, mirroring the glowing city below. Waves lapped softly, light glinting off the surface, merging seamlessly with the gentle luminescence of buildings, streets, and lamplight. Everything seemed at peace, balanced, hopeful.

Yos whispered to himself, a mantra and a promise:

"Dreams don't show us the future. They teach us how to live in the present."

He lifted his gaze to the sky, the distant waters, and felt the quiet joy of belonging—not to a place, not to power, but to truth itself. Dreams had guided him through darkness, betrayal, and despair. Now, they guided him toward light, purpose, and a life shared with those who had once been distant, now close.

As the city's traffic lights shimmered softly beneath him, Yos closed his journal, a serene smile spreading across his face. Around him, friends, allies, and family stood steady. Above, the sky deepened to twilight, calm and infinite, holding promise.

And in that moment, the rooftop felt like the centre of the world—not as a throne, not as a vantage point, but as a place where hope, forgiveness, and dreams could flourish, untamed and free.

And Yos finally understood living in the present was the greatest dream of all.

The rooftop, once lonely and silent, was now alive. And the future—though unknown—was bright with possibility.

Epigraph

Dreams are not an 'escape'—

they are blueprints for courage.

www.ingramcontent.com/pod-product-compliance
Lightning Source LLC
Chambersburg PA
CBHW040529170726
48295CB00012B/392